EXPOSED

JEAN-PHILIPPE BLONDEL

Translated from the French by
ALISON ANDERSON

NEW VESSEL PRESS
NEW YORK

New Vessel Press

www.newvesselpress.com

First published in French in 2018 as *La mise à nu*

Copyright © Libella, Paris, 2018

Translation Copyright © 2019 Alison Anderson

Library of Congress Cataloging-in-Publication Data
Blondel, Jean-Philippe
[La mise à nu, English]
Exposed/ Jean-Philippe Blondel; translation by Alison Anderson
p. cm.
ISBN 978-1-939931-67-2
Library of Congress Control Number 2018963552
I. France—Fiction

The narrator, Louis, is a secondary school teacher, in a lycée in France. For reasons of cultural clarity and consistency I have opted to maintain the French designations for classes in the *collège* and lycée, which run "backward" from *sixième* (sixth class, eleven-year-olds) to *troisième* (third class, fourteen-year-olds) in the *collège* (roughly equivalent to middle school); then *seconde* (second class, fifteen-year-olds), *première* (first, sixteen-year-olds), and *terminale* (final year, seventeen- and eighteen-year-olds) in the lycée. At one point Louis recalls applying to elite preparatory classes at the same time as he applies for university; these elite classes, if successful, grant access to the country's most prestigious, state-run institutes of higher education.

ANTHRACITE

I DIDN'T BELONG THERE. I wandered through the succession of rooms, with a glass of overly acidic champagne in my hand. I looked at the other guests. Their self-confidence, the way they held their heads. Their facial expressions. They formed familiar little clusters, burst out laughing, glanced over at rival groups, occasionally glanced at the canvases, gushed noisily, turned away, murmured a spicy anecdote or scathing commentary into the ear of an acolyte, demolishing the opus they had just praised in the blink of an eye. The men wore jackets that were self-consciously casual. The women in little black dresses shrieked with laughter, and regularly reached up to touch their male partner's arm or shoulder.

A gallery opening, with all its decorum. In fact, it pretty much lived up to the stereotypical image I had of such events. I did not attend this kind of gathering on any regular basis. In my fifty-eight years on this planet I have not, in the end, spent much time in the world of visual arts. This was only the second time I had ever been invited to this sort of occasion. The first time was over a quarter of a century ago. Back then I had gone with a friend who was feverishly exhibiting his work with other local artists. We had hung his paintings ourselves.

Whereas this evening, of course, was different. The painter was local, yes, but his fame had spread all the way to Paris and even abroad. Alexandre Laudin: living proof that art has no regard for either geographical or social origins—he was born and grew up in this provincial town, in a housing development where his parents still lived. But I imagined him comfortably ensconced in the tenth or eleventh arrondissement. Bastille, République. Where the pulse of life beats faster.

Laudin has done the town and its inhabitants proud. He is our cultural guarantor, the reference we like to slip into a conversation, just to show that it is not only in Paris that, etc. His name began to pop up ten years or so ago, if I remember correctly. Ever more frequent articles in the local, then regional and national papers. A discreet but steady ascension. Last week his photograph was on the front page. To announce this exceptional exhibition, a sort of mini-retrospective of five years of pictorial research. The paintings would be on display in this gallery for only two weeks before flying off to Rome, London, or Amsterdam, where admirers were beginning to grow impatient. But before going global, Laudin had insisted on this exhibition in his stronghold. The journalist had emphatically praised his loyalty to his place of birth. The message was clear: Alexandre Laudin, at least, did not think he was God's gift. The opening was on a Friday evening. A private party. By invitation only. I remember smiling as I studied Alexandre Laudin's portrait in the paper. I hardly recognized him. He didn't look like the student I had taught English to, twenty years earlier. I must have had him in *première*, but he made no impression on me. I smiled, the way I did every time I used the verb "to have" to describe the relation between student and teacher. *Monsieur Bichat? I had him in cinquième. You're lucky you didn't have that old bag Aumont.* This is how we define ourselves, us and them. We belong to each other for a few months. Then we set one another free again. We forget one another.

Nowadays, of course, I would notice Alexandre Laudin. On the photographs that appeared in the papers he was staring at the lens with a hard, almost insolent gaze. He exuded money and self-regard. Physically, he seemed to have filled out considerably, whereas I recalled a skinny boy, a scrawny cat in the corridors of the lycée. He must have become an ardent member of gyms and spas. With his shoulder-length hair and three-day stubble he could have been the face of some advertising campaign for men's cologne.

I had been very surprised to find the invitation to the opening in my mailbox. So I was one of the happy few, who nevertheless numbered close to two hundred, by the looks of it. I was flattered, naturally, but puzzled, too. I had rarely run into Alexandre Laudin over the last twenty years, and when I had, we merely nodded knowingly to each other, murmuring some bland pleasantry. We had no desire to hear about each other's lives. I assumed my name had found its way by mistake onto the guest list of the cultural center organizing the event. Flattered or not, I had decided not to go. What was there to gain from that sort of party where I knew no one? I could already imagine standing around alone. How I would feel at loose ends. That I didn't belong. I would rather sprawl on my sofa and read the novel I had started the day before. Or lose myself in the twists and turns of some English TV series about the trials of the aristocracy and their servants at the beginning of the twentieth century.

Yes, but. I'd had a trying day. Célia Richon, in *seconde B*, had been even more unbearable than usual. She scoffed at me with her half smile and rolled her eyes to the ceiling whenever I called her out on something. And of course the head teacher for *seconde B*, who is the phys ed instructor, could not understand how Celia could behave so differently in English class than in gym class. *With me*, the phys ed teacher added, perfidiously, *the girl was adorable.* I was well aware that beneath her carnivorous smile she was questioning my teaching methods, but above all being sarcastic about my age. Maybe it's time to retire? In addition to which I was getting ever more exasperated with my final-year students, who spent all their time trying to sneak glances at their smartphones, and then the arrival in *première littéraire* of a troublemaker expelled from other schools. I couldn't stop sighing, and Isabelle, my philosophy colleague, pointed this out to me. Clearly I had lost my passion, if I'd ever even had any, and with each passing day the effort required to command even a modicum of attention on the part of my students was greater, leaving me exhausted. I worried about the four years of teaching I had left, all the more so as we were in no way sheltered from any new ministerial decrees raising the legal retirement age to sixty-five or even seventy. I had two piles of papers to grade waiting for me, but when I got back to my cold apartment I didn't feel like staying there. I turned the heat up all the way, to hell with saving energy, *après moi le déluge!* The invitation was in plain sight on the living room table. I stuffed it into my coat pocket and went straight back out. On the way I reasoned that at this sort of shindig there was bound to be a mountain of food and that if I went about it carefully I wouldn't even have to make myself dinner. And when I got home it would be so hot in there I'd even be tempted to open a window. Bliss. In the meantime, I was going to stuff myself with hors d'oeuvres.

I observed the crowd. The discreet cracks visible in women's makeup. The traces of cosmetic surgery. The creasing of skin. Fluttering of eyelashes. I heard laughter ringing false. This really wasn't my world. I greatly preferred the anonymity of the movie theaters I often went to on a Sunday: the six p.m. show, so I'd be sure no one would bother me and I could sit peacefully in the third or fourth row, ready to be crushed by the screen and the images I immersed myself in, oblivious to the entire outside world. With films—as with novels, which I devoured with the regularity of a metronome—I gave myself no limits: I fell into every trap the author or director set for me, lost myself with relish in the labyrinths of a fictitious world. I think of that friend of Mary Poppins, the chimney sweep, and the amazing chalk pictures he drew: you could jump into them and become reincarnated. I dreamed of meeting him.

The paintings were no surprise. Over the years I'd seen several reproductions in the local paper and on posters around town. I'd also poked around online, and when the media began to talk about Laudin I'd even checked the website he'd set up to promote his work, a site that disappeared, incidentally, once his success was established.

Tall, gray, almost vertical figures, with touches of bright color. Crowds waiting with anxious expressions for something to happen. A cataclysm. Labored, deformed faces, eyes protruding. A disturbing vision of humanity, reminiscent of both Munch and Francis Bacon, with an incongruous nod to Bernard Buffet, now forgotten; reproductions of his paintings used to decorate our dining room when I was a kid. Enough to freeze the already chilly atmosphere that reigned during family meals.

There were other influences, no doubt, but I didn't want to venture onto the slippery slope of comparison and analysis. My knowledge of art and painting generally was not that extensive. As a body of work it was interesting, but I was aware that the use of that adjective would cause the artist to grind his teeth if ever it were repeated to him. Disturbing, yes, but not really all that innovative. Above all, my gaze slipped over each painting and moved on, never arrested, never lingering. They evoked no emotion, and this was probably deliberate on the artist's part. A cold, harsh world. An exhibition of dystopia. So be it. What bothered me more was that

Alexandre Laudin seemed to be repeating himself lately, the same themes, same use of color, same brushstroke. As if at the dawn of his career he had hesitated on one of the lower rungs of the ladder that would take him toward the sun. I couldn't help but smile at the pompous sentence I'd just voiced mentally. As I made my way through the rooms I ended up in the one farthest from the entrance. It was deserted, and looked out onto a little garden, plunged in darkness. Conversation and laughter from the main gallery area reached the room with a stifled, almost unreal resonance.

"You're smiling, Monsieur Claret?"

I gave a start. There he was, in a corner of the room, leaning against the wall. He came forward, relaxed, lithe, sure of himself, emanating that sort of presence that only success and the prime of one's mid-thirties can give—when an individual is making his way, and trial and error are behind him, and fatigue has not yet set in.

"Do you remember me?"

"Of course I do. How could I not. The papers and the internet keep us regularly informed. What are you doing in here? Shouldn't you be back there in the main room with your guests?"

"I just escaped from there, to be honest. I need a few minutes of peace and quiet before I give my speech."

"Then I'll leave you alone."

"No, stay. I'm glad to see you. Are you doing well?"

"I'm doing, which is already a start. Congratulations on your brilliant career, in any case."

"I guess you never imagined I'd make such a career choice, when I was your student, did you?"

I glanced again at his canvases. Then addressed my reply to them.

"You know, as time goes by you realize you don't really know the adolescents there in the room with you. It's only after they finish the lycée that they really take flight. And make their choices. Their alliances. They rise, fall, struggle to get ahead. But by then, as a rule, we can't help them anymore, because they're no longer in touch. We were only with them for a very short time, over a very short distance. I'm flattered you remember my name."

"I enjoyed your classes."

"That's kind of you. Having said that, I don't think I taught you anything useful where art is concerned."

He waved his hand, as if to brush away my objection.

"No one could have guided me down this path, I don't think. I'd already set off on it a long time before. Oh my God, I sound like I'm giving an interview on the radio, one cliché after another. Forgive me. Whatever the case may be, in your class, I felt safe. As if, during that hour I spent with you, nothing could happen to me. I'm not sure that makes sense."

"Not really, no, but it's always nice to hear. So, apparently your next exhibition will be in Amsterdam?"

"First Madrid. Then the Netherlands. And I have to go to Austria in a few weeks to finalize a project with a gallery. I'm becoming European."

"But you've started with this opening in your hometown. Your loyalty is touching, to use the words of the local paper."

He guffawed and came a few steps closer.

"Let's be honest, it's mainly a way for me to talk big and act big around all these people, here, who used to think I was a complete moron. And it's also a way to honor the local authorities, who have supported me, a lot. And to be sure of that support if I need their help. You know what it's like, the life of an artist. Ups and downs. One day I will go out of fashion, no doubt."

"You're very pessimistic."

"Realistic, rather. It doesn't stop me from making the most of whatever happens. On the contrary, I'd say."

We stood side by side for a moment, facing one of his oldest works. His vertical period, I call it. Towers, crushed people, an absence of sky. I wondered who would buy a painting like that. And where they would hang it once they'd bought it.

"I didn't want them to exhibit the early work, but they insisted. A retrospective only makes sense if you start with the beginning."

"Isn't it a little embarrassing, a retrospective at your age?"

He shrugged and answered that at first, yes, he'd been somewhat surprised, then he got used to the idea, and the project couldn't have come at a better time because, precisely, he needed to move, needed to change his routine, change his palette and even his brushstroke. He'd been absorbed in research over the last few months. Experimenting. He wanted to turn the page. He was telling me this when a tall blonde woman, slender and nervous, walked across the room, according me an almost scornful glance before she addressed Alexandre sharply. With a brusque gesture she pointed to her wristwatch. Laudin nodded. He gave my left shoulder a gentle squeeze. And was gone. A few seconds later there was a burst of exclamations. Applause. The cultural circus. I heard the beginning of his speech. His subtle irony. Brisk sound bites.

It was time for me to head toward the buffet the waiters had just set up. In ten minutes or so the guests would storm the food and it would be virtually impossible to get near the table. I found a strategic position, one that would allow me to both wolf down a few dozen petits fours in record time and then slip away quickly.

I had exchanged a few words with a celebrity. I was about to feed myself at the expense of a city council I had not voted for. A magnificent evening.

For a while, life went on as normal. At the beginning of November, I had dinner with my eldest daughter, who made a quick stop in her hometown on her way to Paris. There she would be meeting one of her physicist colleagues who worked, as she did, on waves and signals. I have never really fully understood what her field of research encompasses or what, exactly, would be the real application of any discovery she might be working on. She tried to familiarize me with the concepts she juggled, but even though I nodded as I followed the movements of her lips, her words made no sense. She would eventually laugh at my glazed eyes, and we'd change the subject. We'd talk about her younger sister, for example, who emigrated to Canada the minute she got her degree in order to be with her current love interest, and she'd found a job in a law office in Montreal. When they were little and I'd be there in the kitchen at five in the morning with the baby sling over my stomach, trying against all odds to get them back to sleep, I often wondered what on earth I'd be able to pass on to them. My passion for books and words that swell, pierce your skin, and cause your throat to dry and the veins

13

on your temples to pound in just a few sentences. My love of music, and those strings of notes that instantaneously evoke a landscape and a season, a restive October sky over the northern plains, the leaden sun of July in the southern swamps. I pictured them as novelists, journalists, playwrights, actors, musicians. I still can't tell whether they chose their professions simply in reaction to my own aspirations or because they really were drawn to them. In any case I was totally off the mark but, as Iris, the youngest, explains, when she condescends to connect on Skype to share her news, the main thing is that now they are headed down the paths that suit them. We know our own children so little, in the end. We know other people so little, in general. All we do is project on them the fantasies they have inspired.

I'd taken down a reproduction of a Modigliani that I'd hastily hung on the living room wall when I moved in and replaced it with the poster for Alexandre Laudin's exhibition. It clashed with the rest of the room, and looked paltry, with no frame or glass to enhance it, but I didn't care. I didn't have many guests and with the ones who did come to visit we often sat in the kitchen because it was light and warm and gave onto the roofs of the neighboring houses. The living room had virtually become a private sphere, an extension of my bedroom.

Now and again I thought back on my conversation with Laudin. I wasn't sorry it had been interrupted. I wouldn't have had the skill necessary to keep the spark of the exchange lit, and we would have both stood there with our arms at our sides, in an awkward silence, the little ash pile of our memories between us. What could a former student and his teacher possibly have to say to each other, once they've dispensed with banal pleasantries about their respective careers, and the passage of time, obviously, leaving its traces on one's face?

When I picked up the telephone that Saturday morning, one month after the exhibition, I thought it would be yet another indefatigable telemarketer wanting to tell me about online banking, funeral contracts, or solar panels. I'd mustered a dose of hostility sufficient to get rid of the intruder, so initially I was thrown by Alexandre Laudin's voice on the line. He was calling from Amsterdam. He was sorry to disturb me, he said, because surely I had a million other things to do, however he wanted to know whether we could meet the next time he was in town. I heard myself say it was a bit unexpected but hey, why not, did he have a more precise idea of when he'd be coming?

"Tomorrow."

I hesitated for a second or two. I suppose part of me thought I ought to make an excuse that I was otherwise engaged, just to show him that my life was not a social wilderness. But on the other hand I was flattered—and intrigued, too. What did Laudin want with an old guy like me? I agreed. Where would he like to meet?

"At my place?"

"Sorry?"

"I have a pied-à-terre there."

He cleared his throat. Started over. Apologized, said he

hated the way he expressed himself—sometimes, he added. In short, he had bought a sort of loft, a little out of the center of town, near the railroad tracks. He'd furnished it just any old way, and the former attic was also a studio, "Well, you'll see, Monsieur Claret. Five p.m., does that work for you?" He was flying back to Paris in the morning and thought he should be back home by early afternoon. He gave an embarrassed laugh.

"You see, I said *back home*. I'm supposed to be living in Paris but I'm still hopelessly provincial."

"Do you have two houses?"

"Two addresses, in any case."

"You know the old saying, 'A second home leads to restlessness syndrome.'"

"I'm basically restless. See you tomorrow, then? I have something I'd like to discuss with you."

"I suppose you do, Alexandre. Otherwise, what would be the point of meeting?"

I could hear him smile over the phone. He probably shook his head. Wise guy, that Claret, all the same. He hung up.

I spent part of the evening going through the cardboard boxes I'd piled up in the storage room after I moved in. They were full of photographs, letters I'd received until e-mail obliterated postal correspondence, newspaper articles about school events from twenty years ago, notebooks one-third filled with thoughts, the beginnings of stories, or ideas I'd forgotten long ago, and useless little items that were supposed to remind me of a particular moment but which no longer evoked a thing—a tiny wooden music box with a clown drawn on it, a cotton sun hat with beige-and-blue stripes, a black-and-white photo of Jack Kerouac cut out of a book I'd stolen from the library ages ago. I haven't been adding anything to this clutter in the last few years, because life has stopped manufacturing memories for me. I rarely go dipping into the mess because I'm not really drawn to the past. Or to the future, for that matter. Only the present really holds my attention and even then, only intermittently. I am the master of a floating world. I let myself drift: come what may. For decades I tried to make the most of the present day, without ever succeeding, then I managed to, inadvertently, after I turned fifty. I live in a state of feeble irony. My colleagues, as a rule, think I am jovial and likeable. The younger ones don't seem to care one way or the other, but imply they would love to be as fit as I am when they reach my age. The only problem, deep down, is that nothing ever moves me any more at all.

I took out the old class photos. The ones where I have pride of place to the right of the group, smiling but focused, while the students try hard to look their best, aware that any imperfection captured that day will be immortalized, and will come back like a leitmotif in future conversations, during the drinking sessions of their twenties, the alcohol-laden gatherings of their thirties, or the late-blooming dinner parties of their forties. There will always be one guest who is only too eager to remind them of how stupid one of them looked, with that old-fashioned shirt, or the horrible haircut of the era, and the others will add fuel to the fire with more or less sordid gossip and anecdotes that are apocryphal at best. Class pictures are the only images that we leave behind of our adolescence in a milieu consisting of neither family nor friends. They are the first evidence of our socialization—or the failure thereof.

Early on in my career as a teacher I collected them, and then one day I stopped. It was in the late 1990s, my daughters were growing fast, life was tugging at me, making demands on me from all sides; I didn't want to be burdened with all those pictures of students who, sooner or later, I would no longer be able to identify. It came, therefore, as a major surprise to realize that, in fact, their names often remained intact in my memory, alongside the faces they had back then.

It took me a good half an hour to find the photograph of the *première littéraire* class of 1996–1997. In the upper left-hand corner Alexandre Laudin was smiling faintly. He was wearing beige and gray clothing that almost blended into the wallpaper of the day students' hall where the photographer had gathered his troops. And as with any group of adolescents, there were clans, and well-defined boundaries. Flamboyant personalities. Small-time rebels. Constant worriers. That girl, for example. Agathe Delange. She suffered from a condition not yet known as "school phobia," and every hour in class was a minor victory over the rampant depression consuming her. She seemed to fade away, standing there next to Baptiste Larmée—who hosted parties everyone dreamed of being invited to—with his long blond forelock, his arrogant, strong blue gaze, shirt open, discreet tattoo on his shoulder ten years before it became all the rage to cover one's skin with draw-ings. I know what has become of many of them. We live in a town of only sixty thousand inhabitants and, as they walk down the pedestrian streets, former teachers will often hear directly from their erstwhile flock—now free and of age—about the circumstances or indiscretions of this or that for-mer student. Baptiste Larmée has changed a lot, apparently, following an automobile accident in which he killed one of his friends. Agathe Delage hasn't done too badly; the last I heard, she was a speech therapist in the Paris suburbs. But when they were posing for the camera, they didn't realize that the secluded world they moved in, with its codes and tacit exclusions, would burst wide open a few months later, and that they would have to dive headfirst into the river of life there before them. When they reach the shore, breath-less, they will look behind them, astonished at how far they have come. The lycée will have vanished, somewhere behind a bend in the river. All that will remain is a muddled impres-sion. A mirage. I stared hard through the years at Alexandre Laudin's face, but I could not decode him. He gave no key. A ghostly presence in a colorful world. I was not able to place him in the mental image of the class I was re-creating. This left me feeling slightly uneasy.

I did have a quick look at other archives after that, of course. I found the faded red cardboard folder that con-tained my administrative papers—diplomas, report cards,

notarized deeds, reports, birth, marriage, and divorce certif-
icates, title to the house, deed of sale of the house—all those
little bundles of paper that sum up the jumble of our lives. A
few Polaroid prints fell out. I'd been one of the last owners of
one of those amazing cameras that offered instant memories
to anyone present, photos to be consumed and forgotten. My
elder daughter at the age of four on a merry-go-round, deadly
serious, astride a wooden steed called Zeus. The younger one
at seven and a half, two canine teeth missing, seated on a red
plastic sled. Photographs took leave of our lives in the mid-
2000s. We did not take as many, because our daughters had
grown and become recalcitrant; they would rather pose for
their friends, and the few pictures we managed to get were
incorporeal now, as they went from cell phone to flash drive
or computer screen. We didn't print them out anymore and
we never got together all four of us to contemplate and discuss the vestiges of our past. Then came the separation and
the move which followed. This was the first time I had rum-
maged around in the storage room, disturbing a collective
memory which now was only individual.

It was after two o'clock in the morning by the time I col-
lapsed on the bed. Outside, Saturday night was dishing up
its portion of car horns, loud shouts, and flashing lights. My
place in the universe. Here and now. Where the story begins.

SULFUR

"So, what do you think?"

Alexandre is blowing on his coffee cup. We are sitting on black leather stools, in a spacious kitchen, separated from the vast living area by a small brick wall which serves as a bar. Large picture windows give onto a balcony, offering a glimpse of the one-way street where I hadn't managed to park. Two bare-branched trees. A paved courtyard.

"It's big."

Alexandre informs me that there are two more rooms, in the "nighttime" area behind us. In addition, he has set up his studio in the attic with a glazed roof, the purpose of which no one can understand anymore in this day and age. The problem is that it gets horribly hot there in the summer, even though the roof has been insulated. The building was once a manor house, in the early twentieth century, one of those opulent dwellings built by a pillar of the textile industry back when spinning mills were booming. The house was split into apartments in the early 1960s. An old lady lives on the ground floor, in an illusion of past splendor. On the second floor, a very discreet family: he is an engineer in the nuclear industry and is often away on business. The children are young adults and are hardly ever at home anymore. I look up and give him a smile.

"Are you proud, Alexandre?"

"Of what?"

"Of having managed to become the owner of the sort of place that is light-years from what you might have aspired to, given your social background?"

His coffee goes down the wrong way. He coughs twice then looks me right in the eye. I can read the words going through his mind, some of them vulgar, others threatening: "Who do you think you are, you old graybeard? Get the hell out of here, asshole!" They give way to a gleam of irony and something very gentle as well.

"Do you remember my parents?"

"Not really. I must have met them during the parent-teacher conferences, but you see so many faces at those events, and none of them really leave their mark, in the end. Still, if you'd been born rich, you wouldn't feel the need to show me around the apartment as if you were a real estate agent."

"You are just as I remember. Ruthless."

"But well-intentioned all the same, I hope. Having said that, you didn't answer my question."

"Proud? I think so, yes. Is there anything wrong with that?"

"Of course not. You didn't trample on anyone to climb the social ladder, as far as I know. That is rare. In any case, no one has the right to judge you."

"Other than critics. The general public. Gallery owners.

Clients. City councils. Local politicians. Journalists. And other artists. They spend their time dissecting me."

"You, or your work?"

"It's the same thing, isn't it?"

"I don't know. I don't know you well at all."

"You really are a strange guy."

"I like the 'really,' and what it implies."

"Sitting here across from you I feel like I'm back in the classroom."

"I'm sorry."

"It's nothing. I already told you they're not unpleasant memories. What did you think of the retrospective the other evening? I looked for you after my speech but you were gone."

"I don't really know much about the visual arts. My opinion is worthless."

"I'm not looking for an expert opinion. I would just like to know what you think of the paintings. How they've developed. Don't worry, I'm not going to wheedle it out of you. Contrary to what you used to do in class."

"Excuse me?"

"You used to torture us, Monsieur Claret! We always had to have an opinion about everything. Of course there were some who were only too glad to speak up, but there were others, like me, who would cringe until we could get back to written work. But you really insisted. You'd go digging in the darkest corners. You'd deliberately call on the ones who stayed silent."

"It's my job. I have to encourage students to express themselves."

"There were times when it was agony."

"I thought you just said you didn't have any unpleasant memories."

Alexandre gives a short, harsh laugh. For a few seconds he practically contorts his body.

"One point for you."

"I hope this isn't a match. Otherwise I'll hang up my gloves right away. I don't know how to fight, and no way am I going to take on a former student."

"Why not?"

A few seconds of silence. An autumn sun angling in through the picture window. In the distance, an airplane taking strangers to an uncertain destination, leaving only a trail melting into the clouds.

"I don't know how to explain it. I think a teacher signs a tacit contract with his students from the moment they walk into the classroom. It goes beyond a pact of nonaggression. It is an agreement that stipulates that even over the years, there will be respect between us, and . . . how should I put it . . . mutual protection. I'm not sure this makes any sense."

"And I doubt whether your feelings would be shared by your colleagues. Or by some of the kids you have there in front of you."

"Leave me to my illusions, Alexandre. I've only got a few more years to run the show."

"You're very good at evading the issue. You still haven't answered my question."

"All right. The first pictures I saw, a few years ago, seemed interesting, disturbing. Crowds. Silent cries. A sort of universal Munch. The second period, too, with those swollen or ravaged faces, even though, once again, what you were seeking was alien to me, because what I am looking for, above all, at this time in my life, is something gentle. A tender lucidity, if you like. No doubt because I'm tired, and feel numb. There's this general dulling of my personality."

"I don't find you particularly dull."

"Because you haven't spent time with me."

"And the next series of paintings? The most recent ones?"

"Are you sure you want to know?"

"Uh-oh."

"You're repeating yourself, Alexandre. You're going around in circles. I don't think that blending your first two periods to come up with a third one is a good idea. It's as if you've hit a wall and you're struggling to get past it. But let me say again that I'm no expert. You'd have to ask for the opinion of someone more qualified than I am, and I'm sure you've already done that."

"No. Neither their opinion nor their advice. I make my own way, that's all. Come what may."

"And that is perfectly fine. Forget what I just told you."

"I certainly won't. Thank you for being so honest."

"But it hurt you."

"No. Yes. It doesn't matter. What I wanted was to hear what you had to say."

"I'm not sure I know what you mean."

"I'm getting to know you. I need to know that feeling. Familiarity. To have some time together, before."

"Before what?"

"I have a favor to ask of you."

"You really are beginning to worry me, young man."

"And there's good reason. But rest assured, I'm not a gerontophile. At least not sexually speaking."

"This is all very unclear, Alexandre."

"Come with me, I have something to show you."

I follow him. The bathroom door is open. I catch a glimpse of my reflection. A man who has aged. A tired man who is trying to hold out against time, but simply can't. We walk past what must be Alexandre's bedroom. An indescribable mess, which clashes with the almost clinical neatness of the rest of the apartment. Another door, across the hall. A large room, dark despite two windows. The blinds have been lowered and let no light in. A stuffy smell. Alexandre hits the switch. A bare bulb. I blink. It takes me a few seconds to get used to the harsh light. When at last my retina has gotten rid of the colored dots, the triptych blows me away.

A woman. A man. The same man and woman, side by side.

Slightly older than I am. Ravaged. Long faces. Dry lips. Bitter lines at the corners of their mouths. They are standing. Stiffly. There is brown. Ochre. A nauseous grayish green that reminds me of beet fields in winter. Or clay. Yes, clay.

She is wearing her Sunday best. She ought to feel proud, and yet she doesn't feel at ease. She would like to scratch her neck and her armpit, but she is rigid. An unpleasant moment to get through. One among many. She is resigned. She hasn't worn this dress in years. Consequently the colors have faded, but what difference does it make, everything is faded, stained by time and earth, since everything has taken on this nauseating hue of rubber boots and rotten meat. A strand of hair has fallen over her forehead and it bothers her. She would like to put it back. Discipline it. Discipline is important. Critical. We all have our place in the world and we have to keep it. To try to rise above it is to go against nature. Obey. That is our lot. There is nothing else to say.

He is wearing a suit. The cut has seen better days; so has he. But he intends to look dapper. Not enough to smile, however. He knows that portraits are important. They are messages for the children who will come after. A testimony to our values. Our humility. Our resistance to change and pretention. Our scorn for smokescreens and castles in the air. Our faith in perseverance and in the procession of immutable days. We will keep our place if we pay this price. All around us the world may crumble, we will go on standing up straight in our boots. Immutable. That is our strength. Our credo.

I step slowly closer. I don't want them to notice me. I would like to touch them. To shake them. To reassure them, too. It is all very confusing. I can sense Alexandre Laudin breathing next to me. Life sometimes takes the most surprising turns. I would never have thought I might find myself one day in an empty room with him, our gazes and our thoughts drawn to the same figures. In this strange, almost unpleasant intimacy.

"My parents."

I am hardly listening. I have begun a silent dialogue with this man and this woman. I think we understand each other. All this energy used up, over so many years, all those evenings spent listening out for the slightest noise, all those nights of fear because a cough, because a wheezing in the chest, because a fever, because an earache, because nightmares. All this time we put ourselves on hold, because they were more important than we were, because they were the next generation, the future, hope, and because we had to protect them, because that was the role incumbent upon us. We may say that the years just sped by, that we hardly had time to get our bearings—in fact they bled us dry, our features drawn, purplish-red patches on our skin and in our memories. Then all of a sudden the house is silent. We go around in circles. We stare at ourselves in the bathroom mirror. We hardly recognize ourselves. Sounds are muffled. How are we going to fill the weeks and months ahead?

We lost each other, Anne and I. We separated less than two years after the girls left home. We hadn't planned it that way. On the contrary. We thought that at last we would be able to spend time together, be ourselves again. We'd planned all sorts of things to do, weekly appointments for meditative activities that would bring us nirvana: qigong, shiatsu, Pilates, Tibetan singing bowls; hours spent learning to paint with watercolors or memorizing text and mime in an amateur theater troupe. And then we would at last be able to devote ourselves fully to our work. All those technological advances that we had set aside for the moment—at last we'd be able to immerse ourselves in them with delight. We did none of that. In any case, not together. To our ironic astonishment, we soon realized that we no longer shared the same aspirations, and that what had initially attracted us to each other—that palpable nervousness, in me, that suspicious meticulousness in her—had become unbearable. By mutual agreement we set each other free, with a great deal of tenderness and respect. We were pleased with what we had accomplished. It was time to turn the page. But I am speaking in her name, when deep down I don't know what she felt. A few months later she met Gauthier, through a now-defunct website that reconnected former classmates. It was with him that she painted, went running, moved, traveled, finally ended up getting involved in permaculture and promoting local business. She is now a stakeholder in a group of activists campaigning for a new economy, more just and respectful of the environment. When I run into her in town she is never on her own; and when we talk over the phone she has always just come back from some meeting or other. She asked me several times to drop in on their sessions; I declined. I don't want to act the needy ex-husband.

Outside, a gust of wind. The rolling blind creaks. I emerge from my active lethargy. The hypnotist is still at my side.

"What did they have to say about it, Alexandre?"

"They don't know. I worked from photographs. Their

31

wedding photos, to be precise. I, uh, I tried to reproduce the picture, integrating the passage of time."

"It's terrifying."

"You think so? Then I'm glad. Even if it means the paintings will never leave this room. In any case, no one has ever seen them."

"When were they made?"

"This summer. I was shut away for hours up there. The heat was unbearable. Everyone had gone on vacation. I was up there on my own alone with them. I started a conversation."

"An indictment, more like."

"No, I don't think so. I hope I've respected them. You think it's too harsh?"

"I don't know your parents."

"That's not an answer."

"Let's just say it's totally uncompromising."

"Thank you."

"Why me, Alexandre?"

I turned to him. His profile in the stark light. A redness at the base of his neck, threatening to spread everywhere, over ears, cheeks, brow, but he manages to contain it by clenching his jaw and narrowing his eyes slightly. I smile. When I brought up his name in the faculty room a few days after the opening, none of the teachers recalled having him in class—twenty years ago most of my colleagues were still students—except for Géraldine Lefèvre, who is due to retire next year, and the first thing she referred to was the disconcerting speed with which Laudin (Géraldine always calls her students by their family name and insists they use the formal *vous* with her) would blush. She taught biology and natural sciences, and the moment an even slightly risqué subject was broached, or whenever she made the unfortunate mistake of berating him for his passive attitude, he turned scarlet. Mentally, she used to call him the Peony. "I'm not surprised, in the end," concluded Géraldine peremptorily, "that he has now devoted himself to color." Appreciative gazes. Silent applause. The faculty room is a miniature stage where each of us tries, at some point, to become a master comedian. When she mentioned Alexandre's last name, I had almost put my finger on a memory. For a split second I had glimpsed him, third seat along, right-hand row. Awkward. Ill at ease. Bright red. And then the doors closed and the image receded into the depths of my memory. Laudin remained an enigma. I couldn't place him.

His neck returns to its normal color—a near-white beige. He murmurs, "I think you may have already guessed." He's right, but I want to hear him confirm it to me. It seems so unlikely.

"You want to paint my portrait?"

He swings around. He is facing me. This time, he lets the purple take over. The hue spreads progressively, rising up his Adam's apple, taking on his chin and nose then fanning out all the way to the roots of his hair.

"I really would like to, yes."

In the few seconds that follow, we gaze into each other's eyes. His are a motionless, deceptive pool. The blue is almost metallic.

"I don't see why."

"Nor do I, Monsieur Claret. I think the reasons behind this urge will come to me gradually. Or once I've finished the canvas. Or never. I suppose that is not a satisfactory answer."

"It's honest, at least."

"All I can say is that when I saw you the other day, I understood that you had played an important role in my life. I thought about you all evening, part of the night, and all of the following week. You became an obsession."

"Now you're scaring me."

"This happens a lot. But there's nothing to be afraid of."

"I'm not as sure as you are, now that I've seen those portraits."

"You're not my father."

"I'll think about it."

"There's something about you that I find moving. A pitiful argument, I know."

"And in your parents?"

"In them, too, yes. But my irritation was stronger. And on top of it, my fear of their death. I'm confused, aren't I?"

He had stopped blushing. I've never been prone to that type of physical reaction. I wonder how far the color spreads—top of the chest, shoulders, forearms? An incongruous thing to wonder if ever there was one, but my mind was buzzing with questions.

"I'm a little thrown. I'm going to head home."

"Of course. Before you go, let me clarify a few things, so that you can make your decision in full knowledge of the facts. I won't work from photographs this time. I would like to go back to a certain ... how to put it ... classicism. To periods of calm. Concentration. Natural light. Using oil. I think I'll even make some of my own pigments. The brown, in particular. The canvases, twenty-four by thirty-six. Not too big. Or too crowded. We'll work in the studio. I want space. You'll sit on one of the living room chairs. With that ordinary sweater you were wearing the other day. Gray. Anthracite. You know the one?"

"I haven't said yes yet."

He's not really listening. He sighs. His shoulders droop. He explains that naturally it will mean sittings. Long. Tiring. You cannot imagine how sore you get when you're obliged to stay three or four hours without moving. And besides, maybe I don't have time for him. But it would be a pity, wouldn't it? Because we would have the time to talk, to get to know each other. He adds that he doesn't need long stretches of silence. What he wants, above all, is for things to feel natural. Familiar. And the essence. The essence of the other person. Yes, the essence of the other person. He nods his head several times. I think of Pinocchio in Geppetto's workshop. I reach for my coat. I promise I'll be in touch soon. This time, when my eyes meet his, I tremble. The pool has vanished into a deep abyss. All that is left is a trace of water. Washed out. Sunken.

I stand for a few minutes at the entrance to the building, confounded. I have not been through such a maelstrom of contradictory emotions in years. Since the birth of my daughters, perhaps. Or even before then. I walk along the sidewalk. I'm having trouble returning to the everyday. But I don't think that's a bad thing. Inside me, in my rib cage, there's a throbbing the likes of which I've rarely known. I feel as if I'm walking along a narrow footpath on the side of a mountain. And oddly enough, I'm not afraid.

I know I will say yes.

"ARE YOU COMFORTABLE?"

I can't help but laugh. I'm sitting on a white wooden chair, in the middle of an empty room where the floor has been covered with a huge plastic tarp. Through the glass roof filters a wan, early November light. Outside, gray clouds pursue one another and fuse now and again into a violent downpour.

"Don't hesitate to let me know if you need anything."

"I feel like I'm in the hospital with a nurse who is swamped with work but thoughtful all the same."

"I'm as intimidated as you are, Monsieur Claret."

"Can I ask you a favor?"

"Anything you like."

"Drop the Monsieur. My name is Louis."

"I don't think I can."

"Of course you can. I know how proud former students feel when at last they can use their teachers' first names."

"I'll try."

"How should I sit?"

"Straight. I think. I'll be trying hard to figure out the best approach, you know. I'm sorry. I hope I won't waste your time. In any case, I won't torture you. Let me know when you've had enough."

"You haven't got a brush, or a palette, or a canvas. You're an odd sort of painter."

"I'm just going to do some sketches for the time being. I'll use wax crayons to fill in the colors. I . . . I'll sit right across from you, if you don't mind."

He takes a chair like the one I'm sitting on, and crosses his legs. I smile.

"This is very intimate, don't you think?"

"That is probably what is most troubling. This closeness. This detailed observation. Being stared at. Dissected. More than what will end up in the painting itself. You can still say no, Monsieur . . . I mean, Louis."

"I agreed to these tacit conditions."

"Thank you. I'm very touched."

"By the way, I still don't really understand exactly why I agreed. But I'll shut up, I'm sure you need to concentrate."

"Oh, no, not at all. I'd rather we spoke. I need flow. The situation is already so artificial. And besides, that way I'll get to know you, bit by bit."

"Expose me, you mean, Alexandre."

I expect him to blush again, but he doesn't. He raises his head and looks me straight in the eye. Deep in his pupils there is an insolence and cruelty I have never seen. His voice is clear when he replies, yes, that's exactly what he is doing. And for that reason I can still say no. Now or at any moment, if I think it's not really worth the effort, or if I'm revealing more than I would like. He is going to search me, dig deep, find what is hidden beneath the doormats of my memory and my body. He gives a short laugh and adds that it's enough to make anyone want to run off when they hear him, when in fact it's just the opposite he wants. My stillness. My truth. Outside, a sudden gust, stronger than all the others. The window panes rattle. His gaze slips away for a few seconds and when it settles on me again it has lost its brilliance. Instead, there is gentleness. A sea of gentleness.

"I used to draw you a lot, when I was a student."

He takes the charcoal and the sketchbook from the bar. The faint squeaking of pencil on paper. A shiver rises slowly from my lower back to my neck. Alexandre's eyes darting back and forth from my body to his fingers. He is absorbed in his task. I take a deep breath. I would like to regain some serenity. I lose myself in gazing at the wall beyond Alexandre's shoulder. Gradually the angles grow softer. There are little spots of light before my eyes. Phosphorescent specks of dust. Colors are born. The purple of heather clinging to rocks. Lichen spreading across the stone, making it plantlike. In the distance, the curve of a loch. The wind blowing along the sides of the car, gusting inside now and again. The hiss of tires on the still damp road. The shower has passed, saturating colors. It's magnificent. Takes my breath away.

*Arnaud's profile. The ridge of his nose. His piercing gaze, try-
ing to take in the landscape. We were all alone, for miles around.
It was early June. He'd rung at the door of the studio where I
was living, on my own since Nina had decided to slam the door
on me a few weeks earlier. He was nervous. Couldn't stand still.
He felt as if he were banging up against the confining walls of the
life that lay ahead of him, walls he hadn't chosen. A girlfriend
he was tiring of, whereas she wanted to make their relationship
official. A profession as a dentist that he'd slaved away to secure,
and now he was beginning to suspect it would bring him nothing but frustration. Parents who had fled Franco's Spain in the
1960s and who expected him to fulfill all the dreams they'd had
to abandon. On the tiny sofa of my tiny apartment he told me
how every night he would wake up in a sweat. He needed air,
space, distance. His anxiety grew as the day went by. He was
filling in for someone in our hometown for three weeks. Then he
was supposed to head north, to Hénin-Beaumont, where another
dental office awaited him, because one of the dentists would be
out on maternity leave. So for a year or two he'd be working
on short-term contracts, then he'd meet with the banks, take*

*out a few loans, and for two decades he'd be in chains. He was
beginning to understand why so many dentists were depressed or
alcoholics. He was thirsty. He wanted some vodka. I drowned
it in orange juice. To change the subject I asked him where he
would like to be at that very moment. He made a face. The obvious answers: New York, Las Vegas, Rio. Then a faint, blasé smile
which meant, with him, that he was about to tell me a secret.
"Scotland," he murmured. "Anywhere in Scotland. When I was
in sixième, I collected those laminated pictures they gave you in
boxes of chocolate powder. The series was called 'Our Beautiful
World.' There was one I really liked. A sort of wild landscape.
A road winding through the Highlands. Toward the bottom,
a lake. I'd stuck it on the front page of my English notebook.
Whenever the teacher started losing her temper and began to
yell I'd find refuge in the photograph, to still my beating heart.
Everything around me would vanish. It was magical."*

"And you never went there? It's not all that far, after all."

*Arnaud shrugged. Gave a grunt. Work. Routine. Daily life.
His fiancée dreamed only of America. I didn't let him finish his
sentence. I stood up. I said, "Let's go," and in Arnaud's eyes there
was confusion and a vague fear. "Where?" "Scotland, obviously.
I'll take sweaters for us both." I had begun hastily stuffing a few
things in my backpack. "Have you got your ID on you? I have
some money. We can change it on the ferry." All Arnaud could
come out with was, "But why?" And I didn't have any satisfactory explanation for him. Nothing, other than the prospect
of another solitary, depressing weekend, stuck between the two
skylights of my studio. Of a well grounded life, where nothing*

would skid out of control. When I turned the key in the ignition, the car clock said it was nine p.m. Arnaud was speechless. I was not the sort of guy who took the initiative, as a rule. I had a tendency to just go with the flow. We stopped at an autoroute rest area to eat some sandwiches and chips. The red and yellow lights of the service station lit up a nocturnal world we had forgotten about. In the middle of the night we took the ferry. I slept on the leatherette seat, my head touching Arnaud's knees. When I woke up the first thing I saw was his smile.

On Saturday evening we were walking exhausted, ecstatic, through the streets of Edinburgh. We knew that at best we wouldn't be home until Tuesday, but it didn't matter a bit. Arnaud was between two contracts. I would leave a brief message for my superiors, at the collège where I'd been teaching since the beginning of the school year—an urgent family matter, a temporary unavailability, I'd make up the hours later on, again, sorry for the inconvenience. As we left the pub where we'd downed more pints than we could count, Arnaud rammed his hands into the pockets of his jacket and shouted, "A life like this!" Once again we were on the road to adventure we had turned our backs on. We were twenty-five years old. The soundtrack to the 1980s was a clamor of dirty money. I had dreamed of being Kerouac, on the road, out to meet people whose lives intersected with mine, who had things in common with me. Arnaud had seen himself as a radical libertarian. We were sufficiently realistic to understand that this escapade would surely be nothing more than a brief foray off the paths we were on, but we wanted to believe that it was a fresh beginning. And that everything was *still possible. We could not know that a few years later I would meet Anne at an impromptu party in the loft of a former theater or that she would quickly become pregnant, foiling all our game plans, changing all our prospects. It was also impossible to know that, six months after Pauline's birth, Arnaud would settle down at last, buy the eighth-floor apartment he'd had his eye on for some time, or that during the housewarming party, which I couldn't attend because my daughter was sick, he would succumb to a brief psychotic disorder and, suddenly convinced he could fly, would leap off his new balcony.*

For now, it is Sunday.

Sunday morning.

We left the youth hostel very early. We have decided not to follow the map. We are headed north. When I run my fingers over my face I can feel my beard reclaiming its rights. We stop at the top of a high, jagged hill, almost a mountain. Below us there is a loch, we don't know the name of it. Clouds go scudding toward the sea. No one for miles around. Orange. Brown. Mauve. Lichen, rocks, heather. A smile spreads across Arnaud's face. He murmurs: "There it is." He murmurs: "Listen." He has rolled down the windows and switched off the engine. He releases the hand brake. As we begin to roll down the steep slope, the only sound is that of the wind whistling into the car, causing the windshield to vibrate. My stomach is in a knot and my eyes open wide to take in the landscape. When the tears come, I don't know if they are from the harsh slap of wind or the beauty of the world. Part of me stays there, suspended, forever.

I MOVE MY CHAIR BACK A FEW INCHES. I rub my eyes. All of a sudden I'm exhausted. I reread the lines I've just written in this notebook I bought in haste on my way back from Alexandre's place. I'm flabbergasted. It's been years since I've written anything other than lesson plans and to-do lists. As an adolescent I used to write. I remember a diary, which probably didn't last more than a few months and which got lost during one of my moves. Two or three short stories of a vaguely fantasy genre when I first discovered the famous dystopian works. The start of a novel, ten or twenty pages, and then the rapid conviction that the story would never get off the ground and that I wasn't meant to be a writer. I put the cap on the pen. Writing by hand. That, too, is surprising. For someone like me who swears by keyboards. There is a cramp in my shoulder I had long forgotten.

For the first time I need to step back and look at what has just happened to me. Normally I am planted firmly on the ground, I lower my head, stretch my neck, and get on with it. But there in the studio it felt very different. It was nothing to do with a problem to be solved or a gap to be filled. There was this pervasive gentleness. In the images that came back to me, like those tree trunks that have lain buried for years at the bottom of a loch and, suddenly freed of their own weight, rise one last time in a whirlwind of bubbles and emerge to trouble the surface before disintegrating for good. It was very strange. I knew I was in Alexandre Laudin's studio. That he was drawing my face from every angle with broad strokes of his charcoal. That I was fifty-eight years old. That I was divorced, the father of two adult daughters. That I had been teaching English for over thirty-five years. I was aware of the white wall in front of me. The bright light reflected by the glass door. And yet I was not altogether there. I saw Arnaud. I was sure that if I moved my hands a few inches I would touch him. His arm. His skin.

All I have found is paper and this blue ballpoint pen to try to keep him here a bit longer. But words don't have the same strength and they give life only to a ghostly sensation. I am haunted. I'm eager to go back to Laudin's studio to see if I can conjure the spirits again, while he tries to steal my features.

My cell phone vibrates. It's Iris, my younger daughter. She is calling for news, and asks me to connect on Skype. Her face on the screen. She is sitting at her desk, in the tiny apartment she gave me a virtual tour of, the other day. She apologizes for her outfit, she's wearing a sweat suit. She just went running in town with her boyfriend. It's ten in the morning in Montreal. Yes, her job is okay, it's not as exciting as she would have liked, but oh well. She uses her English a lot with her colleagues in Toronto and Ottawa. She assures me she has become completely bilingual. She's sure she speaks better than I do, now. I don't doubt it for a moment. Unlike most of my colleagues, I never spent an entire year in an English-speaking country. Posts for language teaching assistants were few and far between. I was attached to my town and my friends. I needed money and independence. I sat the various exams to get my accreditation from the Éducation Nationale and I passed. I never thought there might be a problem. Only later did I begin to feel a certain inadequacy. Iris wants to know how I spent my Sunday. I shrug. Nothing special. She sighs. She adds that I have to make an effort, after all. I bristle.

"What do you mean?"

"I don't know—get out and do things, the way *Maman* does. Meet people. It's no good staying home and brooding all on your own."

"I'm not brooding, Iris. I'm in great shape."

"That's not what Pauline said. She thought you seemed depressed, the last time she saw you."

"You know your sister. She talks all the time and then she complains when others are quiet."

Iris laughs, inside the screen. All you have to do is mention the rivalry between the sisters to change the subject. It's a strategy that never fails. We chat for a few more minutes. I don't mention Alexandre Laudin. Nor does she share anything about her love life, her pain, or joy. We let the details of everyday life wash over us, as they engulf our deepest concerns.

We merely smile, resort to derision and tender irony. As the years go by, we are less willing to encroach upon the other's private sphere. We stay at the door of our respective homes, through the intermediary of our screens. I have long forgotten the scent of her hair. But when the conversation ends on a final burst of forced laughter and the screen goes black, the years swoop down on me. I am about to make myself a coffee when another vibration interrupts my train of thought. All these new sensations that have replaced the sound of a doorbell, or the ringing of a landline . . . I do my best to integrate the latest technology into my personal and professional life. I haven't been altogether successful. Sometimes I find myself wishing that progress would come to a sudden halt and we'd be tossed onto a virgin shore, stunned, at a loss. That cameras would go back to film. That selfies would vanish in favor of portraits slowly drawn by hand with pencil or oil paint.

Alexandre Laudin's name on the screen. I answer mechanically. He is back sooner than he thought. The problem is that he hates dining alone on Sunday evenings. Would I join him at the restaurant?

"Am I your stopgap, Alexandre?"

His laughter down the line. Of course I accept. What else could I do?

We are in one of those Asian cafeterias that over the last twenty years have sprung up in shopping malls on the outskirts of town. Outside, deserted parking lots. Shopping carts shuddering in the onslaught of the wind. An icy, early November darkness. Inside, a couple in their sixties and their toy dog. The wife is wearing a lot of makeup and is nibbling at the selection of stir-fried vegetables she took from the buffet. The husband is stuffing his face with all the fried specialties he could find. A bit farther away is a family, or what's left of it. All four members are glued to their respective smartphones. The screens are reflected on their faces. They've hardly touched their food. They are already virtual. The loudspeakers are crackling with pseudo-Japanese versions of Edith Piaf hits.

"Strange place."

"On Sunday evening, there's not much choice, Monsieur Claret. Louis, I mean. And besides, I'm rather partial to this sort of place. I find them very inspiring."

"That reflects what you paint. If the end of the world suddenly came while we were sitting here, no one would see anything wrong with it."

"Not even you?"

He doesn't leave me time to answer. He explains that in fact these non-restaurants are very restful. No obsequious waiters or owners forcing you to try the local plonk. No risk, either, of running into a client who might recognize you and embarrass you with insistent staring or an ill-timed joke. Complete anonymity. In a provincial town, that is a rare commodity.

"Speak for yourself, Alexandre."

"I am sure you share my opinion. After all, you've been teaching here for a long time, haven't you?"

"More than thirty-five years."

"And you wouldn't want to be within earshot of a colleague or a former student. To have your peace and quiet disturbed all of a sudden."

"You are one of my former students. I'm not afraid of anyone who attended my classes. I'm often glad to have news of them. What would be more vexing would be to run into a student who has to put up with me in class at the moment."

A silence scarcely interrupted by a shrill voice hammering out Piaf's *L'Hymne à l'amour*. A faint smile flickers on Laudin's lips.

"I'm sure they're as enthralled as I was."

"I'm sure they're not. But that's not the issue."

"I liked hearing your voice. I was amazed, too, by your gift for repartee. You managed to reduce every single rooster in the farmyard to silence."

"It's not that hard, really, when you're the farmer."

"That kid, for example . . . Baptiste Something-or-other. Arrogant, with a ravaging smile."

"Larmée. Baptiste Larmée."

"That's him. The sort of kid you remember, I suppose."

"I remember the first and last name of nearly all my students. The problem is that they are stuck with their adolescent face and figure; so sometimes when I see them again I have trouble placing them because they no longer look like themselves. Take yourself. You don't have much in common anymore with who you were."

Laudin's skin begins to molt, turning bright crimson. I add, "Other than your tendency to blush over nothing, naturally," and this time he bursts out laughing and the purple hue fades. He murmurs that he knew he'd have an enjoyable evening. I ask him whether he invited me just to enliven his solitary meal, which I wouldn't really mind, in the end. He shakes his head.

"It's part of the creative process. Yesterday we started talking and then you were absorbed in gazing at the wall and I lost you. I didn't want to disturb you. It was very striking. Do you meditate?"

"No. I was just tired, I think. You know, old people like me, it doesn't take much for us to switch off. But you were talking about Baptiste Larmée."

"One day you called on him because you could tell he wasn't listening to a word you were saying. And he muttered, 'Jeez, piss off,' and you heard it, so you stood right in front of him and said that not only was it your role to call on him but that on top of it you got paid for it. I really admired that. I dreamed of crucifying that bastard."

"You're still angry."

"Yes, it's surprising, isn't it? And here I claim not to give a damn about the past, and I'm drawn to the future, and it's the future that fascinates me. Proclaiming loud and clear that I have no memories of my teen-age years."

"I read that, yes. And also that you were too absorbed by your inner world back in those days, and that it cut you off from other people. I almost believed you."

"The bullshit you have to feed the press, sometimes . . . To make your career seem epic. To show off. And so they'll leave you alone."

"Have you ever thought about psychoanalysis?"

"Of course I have. But I'm afraid of the impact it might have on inspiration."

"That's ridiculous, you know. I'm sure after a few sessions you'd be rid of Baptiste Larmée. What did he do to you, anyway?"

"Oh, nothing, really. Minor humiliations. Unconscious harassment. For him and his clique I didn't exist. They would throw parties and I was never invited. Then they would talk about them openly in my presence. Gratify me with every detail. What happened before. And after."

"You didn't have to stay and listen."

"I know. I figured that at some point they would notice me. Let me into their circle. I dreamed about it for nights on end, knowing very well that it would never happen."

Alexandre Laudin looks over at the next table: the head of the smartphone family has just announced it is time to leave. When Alexandre turns back to face me, the wings of his nose are no longer quivering, and the wave of moisture that nearly darkened his gaze has vanished. Those are all the things that teachers don't notice, even though they're convinced they know their students inside out. The grudges, the attachments that gradually change our trajectories and take us very far from the path we thought we were on. Here, for example, in this warehouse transformed into a temple to Asian industrial cuisine, on a Sunday evening, in the company of a stubborn, distraught, former student. A strange association.

Alexandre clears his throat and asks me to excuse him. "It's ridiculous," he adds. He hasn't thought about it for years, but the simple fact of calmly talking with me brought to the surface something that should have remained buried. All the more so since the lycée was hardly a penal colony. These little vexations certainly formed his character and he would not have become who he is now without these pitfalls. I reply that I have never believed that pain makes us stronger. On the contrary. In my opinion, it is the words of love we receive that strengthen us. He shakes his head and murmurs that I am priceless.

"For the painting, Louis, I . . ."

"Have you already started it?"

"No. That is, I . . . I've done more sketches. There's one I particularly like, but I don't know yet where it will take me. When can you come back?"

"You're the star, Alexandre. You're the one going from one end of Europe to the other. I just stay put, you know. I'm a sort of standing stone. I mark the territory."

"I'll be around more in the coming weeks. I'm going to forsake Paris. For you."

"For me or for you?"

"We are connected, for a time."

"I'll give you my schedule. I work mainly in the morning. My afternoons are free. One of the perks of age. I expect that should suit you."

"And what about grading papers and preparing for class?"

"I'll get less sleep. I don't sleep much as it is."

"You ... You do know that these pictures will be exhibited?"

"Ah ... So there will be more than one, that means."

"I think so, yes. I ... In my mind I see them as a series. One with a yellow background to start with. Rather pale. Sulfur. Another, brown. Or gray. Maybe a third in reddish tones. But the initial layers disappear. And it is all meant to evolve. I'm still feeling my way. I suppose it must seem very muddled to you, and I'm aware of the inconvenience it will cause."

"It doesn't matter."

"I can't get over it."

"Excuse me?"

"This gift you are giving me. The ease with which things are falling into place."

"A few years ago it would have been complicated or even impossible. Well, we really ought to head to the buffet now."

A few years ago, no. Of course not. I saw my life as an obstacle course and myself as an athlete of everyday life, juggling the constraints of my job, my daughters' upbringing, my desire to maintain my friendships, and the slots of time I could devote to reading. Bit by bit it all crumbled away. What is left are long stretches of time where I gaze at the covers of novels I bought and which I rarely even open. My horizons have expanded, but my life has shrunk. It's not a paradox. It's a fate we all share. When constraints begin to fade, we don't know how to fill our new freedom.

What's left are sources of light. Memories drawing a path across the earth. Sometimes, one of these coils of memory becomes more luminous than the others. Almost phosphorescent. A glowworm in a graveyard of memories. Since seeing Alexandre Laudin again, I have been striving to tame them. To admire the way they shimmer and glint. And to catch them.

*I*t was a beautiful week, the weather unusually warm for late October. The girls and I went swimming twice, under Anne's watchful eye. She's an inland person, and had never had the opportunity to spend time by the sea until we took our first vacation there a few years ago. It's an element she's wary of; it has remained foreign to her. She talks about tide pools, currents, tidal ranges, and the late-fall absence of lifeguards. She is right, of course, but we don't listen. We love the power of the waves knocking us off our feet, sometimes hurtling us onto the sand. When we confront the waves, they give rise to a feeling—intrinsically tied to our fear—of pride, and the incredible sensation of being fully alive.

This is our last evening in the village; it empties of people the moment summer folds its parasols. Tomorrow we'll hand in the keys to our rental and drive the five hundred miles from the resort to the town where we live. We never switched on the tiny television. Pauline feels like reading her bestseller, with its story of the drastic choices people are sometimes forced to make when they grow up in a country at war. Anne makes a list of the things we have to do when we get home. Iris is bored. The *wind picked up in the afternoon and drove us indoors to blankets and sofas. Night fell suddenly. It is only nine o'clock, but the resort is deserted. Even the gaggles of children who came for their Halloween treats have abandoned their quest. I suggest going for a walk along the waterfront. Anne frowns. The forecast is for a storm along the coast in the middle of the night, maybe it would be wiser not to go out. Iris emerges from her silence. She promises we won't be long. Just a quick walk.*

The streets of the little town are deserted. The pine trees are bending to the wind. Hunched over, we head toward the ocean. We have decided to take the path overlooking the beach. We hold each other firmly by the arm. The gusts lash us, take our breath away. My daughter is in raptures. I remember an excursion with my parents to the Pyrenees when I was eight years old. We were surrounded by mist as we were walking up a steep slope. My father's curt orders. Sit down. Don't move. Wait for the fog to lift and for the visibility to return. Grin and bear it. It could last a long time. My heart pounding in my chest. The impression that I could reach out and touch something extraordinary. Risk. Danger.

Iris snuggles against me. Her hair flying in the wind. A gust makes her lose her balance. She can't help laughing. A peal of laughter rising on fragile notes, drawn up by columns of air, becoming tiny bubbles of storm. We struggle on, our feet pressed firmly against the earth, our fists in our coat pockets, and as the minutes go by, one by one, my daughter's laughter deepens. It starts at her navel, runs up through her body, emerges in a gush. Her mirth comes over me, I double over so as not to fly away. It is my fear and my secret desire. A kite. A wisp of straw. To be weightless. Then vanish, suddenly, torn apart by currents.

Below us the ocean has gone wild. Dark gray clouds roll past, rare patches of clear sky allow a glimpse of the imperturbable stars. We stand there, exhausted, but on our feet. We are struggling, my daughter and I, to put down roots. And we are laughing. Yes, laughing.

ON CLOSING THE NOTEBOOK, I feel a cramp between my thumb and index finger. I make a few movements—stretch my back, bring my shoulder blades closer together, force myself to breathe deeply—and I hesitate to call her. I quickly work out the time difference—in any case, part of me has always been aware of the time on the East Coast, ever since she moved there. So it's late afternoon where she is. She comes home from work, sends her high heels flying to the far side of her tiny apartment, one of them bounces off the wall and takes a tiny chip of paint with it. She swears. She's not thinking about me. Or about the ocean. Or the wind. She is in another setting. If I contact her with my tales of laughter on the beach she'll get annoyed, she'll reproach me for constantly wallowing in my own mud instead of forging ahead, then she'll frown, worry, are you sure you're all right?

Yes, of course, I'm sure I'm all right. Never been better, not in a long time. She wouldn't understand. I'd have to talk about Laudin, the cheap Asian restaurants, the rice wine we drink, how we make fun of people, imitate them—clients, students, competitors, colleagues—our bodies bent double with laughter on the deserted parking lot, the taxi we had to call because we weren't in a fit state to drive, my dry mouth at night, reminding me of the old days, my head heavy the next morning, and the irritation in my sinuses that makes me less patient, more brusque in class. And the miraculous effect of it: the students fall silent, suddenly surprised and respectful. But I couldn't tell her all that. She'd frown. Wonder about too many things. She'd call her sister. Then her mother. She would share her suspicions. Making headway doesn't mean hanging out with a man who could be your own son. It means joining associations, seeing people who are nearly sixty, and comparing the social prowess of your offspring. It means using faded, watercolored tones—you stop smoking, do low-impact workouts at the gym, drink a glass of good red wine from time to time, fair enough, and while you're at it, why not join a book club at the local library?

There comes a day when your children can no longer be your confidants. There's too much at stake. Too much anxiety. Accumulated frustration. Love, awkwardly expressed.

I decide not to correct the small pile of homework waiting on my desk and I send a message to Damien, whom I still refer to as my best friend even though we haven't done anything together for years, haven't invited each other over since my divorce, and we see each other only very rarely. The last time was four or five months ago. We had planned to meet at a restaurant but as usual our plans fell through: his son showed up unexpectedly, he wasn't doing well, Damien wanted to stay with him. Since then, radio silence.

He answers almost immediately. He's glad to hear from me. He didn't dare call me after all those missed appointments. He was ashamed. Particularly as in the meantime he found out that his son, who'd been practically blackmailing him with threats of suicide, actually had only one real goal in mind: to get as much money out of him as possible. Anyway. What about me? I type one sentence: "Instead of sending texts, we could meet." Twenty minutes later he's ringing the buzzer downstairs. He tells me that he's been going for long walks through town lately. Sometimes he even finds himself all the way on the edge of the residential area. Walking through town helps him clear his mind, because it's pretty confused up there these days. Must be because he's about to turn sixty. Do I feel like joining him?

As we walk past the hospital, on our way to the outskirts—bungalows from the 1930s, workers' allotments, brick school buildings—he tells me he never thought, when he was younger, that he'd reach this age. And now that he is facing the fait accompli, he wonders how he has managed to live for so long. "But the real question, you know, Louis, the real question is: When do we stop, when do we sit down to catch our breath and think about who we really are and what we want, in the end? We spend our time avoiding questions like this. We let ourselves get caught up in this sort of artificial circuit we create for ourselves, from scratch, just to give ourselves the illusion we belong to the human race. Well, anyway, I'm boring you, the way I go on, aren't I? Tell me what you've been doing with yourself. You *what*? You're being painted? What the hell is going on?"

"Do you smoke, Louis?"

Alexandre tilts his head to the left, stretches his neck, then massages his wrists. I notice a bump on the joint between his fingers, probably the relic of a nocturnal fist-fight. I don't ask.

"Actually, I think we know each other well enough now where we could say *tu* to each other, Alexandre."

"I don't think I can. It's as if there's still a desk between us."

"You've taken a fine revenge. You're the one holding the reins nowadays. But, yes, I do smoke, much to my doctor's displeasure, and he warned me that I was bound to die before the end of my next decade."

"I wasn't interrogating you. Just asking politely if I could bum one off you."

"I was sure you didn't smoke."

"I don't. I tried it for a while when I was a student, not inhaling, but I knew right away it wasn't my thing. I like things that allow me to breathe, not what stops me. Whatever opens my lungs. I go running twice a week. I go regularly to the swimming pool. I need sports, so that I won't get all stiff. Painters suffer as much as their models do during sittings."

"Then I won't encourage your vice."

"But you will give me one."

"You're feeling rebellious?"

"From time to time I have to act the part of the stereotypical artist. Come with me, we'll be more comfortable in my bedroom."

"Sorry?"

"There's a balcony overlooking a little garden. It's not possible to open the glass roof. I already tried. I cut myself."

The litany of surprises life has in store. I hadn't planned to stay rooted in this provincial town. Or to become a dinosaur at the school where I teach. Or to have daughters. Or for them to get old. Or for them to go away. Or to divorce. Let alone to find myself leaning on my elbows on a balcony outside a former student's bedroom, smoking, shivering in this mid-November grayness.

"Did you have a look at the painting on your way in?"

"No. I'd rather wait for the finished product. Same with my students' work, if you recall. I don't go up and down between the desks to spy on them while they're writing. I think it's indecent."

"Actually I'm circling around you. I'm sorry, I can't think of any other way to put it. I've done one sketch after the other. I've got the position, the liveliness in your gaze, the mobility in your features, but I've come up against the problem of the colors. I'll be honest, in your absence I already finished two little paintings, eight by eight, but I threw them out. The essential just wasn't there."

"Which means?"

He shrugs. He is holding his cigarette between his index and middle finger, awkwardly. A pose he can't seem to adopt. He mumbles that, in a way, the point is to capture the soul, isn't it? Except that "capture" is a violent verb, and his gestures and method are gentle. "And the soul, what do we know about the soul, anyway? It's a term that disintegrates the moment you try to define it. There are no words, you see, and yet there are plenty of examples. *The Girl with the Pearl Earring.* Van Gogh's self-portraits. Gainsborough. David Hockney's terrifying *Mr. and Mrs. Clark and Percy.*"

"Why is it terrifying?"

"I spent hours looking at it. Here's this couple who don't love each other anymore, and they're staring at the painter, and beyond, at the future viewers. They've only just started hating each other. They hope they'll be able to walk away from it with their heads held high. It's incredible. You've never seen that painting? It's in the Tate Gallery. Don't you ever go there with your students?"

"I don't organize class trips anymore. I'm too old. And when I did, I tended to take the kids to the British Museum or Buckingham Palace. The National Gallery, too. I thought they wouldn't really be into modern art. Maybe I was wrong."

"But you went there at least once."

"Sorry?"

"When I was in *première.* The Tate Gallery was on the

program. I didn't sign up for the trip, of course. I wouldn't have fit in, in any of those cliques that were already formed. I could just imagine the trip on the bus. Ten hours with no one sitting next to me, while the others were singing their heads off, in the back. The face some of them would make at the thought of sharing their dormitory with me."

"You're exaggerating, Alexandre."

I could hear myself saying *vous* to him again. Trying to create a certain distance. I am troubled by the incoherence in my pronouns; he doesn't notice. He goes on, his gaze lost in contemplation of the deserted garden below us.

"I suppose. Maybe it would have been fine. Fun, even. But I wouldn't have had the courage to face the slightest additional humiliation. I protected myself. I didn't even mention the trip to my parents. Particularly as they would probably have said yes. They were afraid of their son. Of his isolation. As incredible as it might seem, they encouraged me to go out. In short, while you were away, I found myself along with a dozen other excluded students haunting ghostly classrooms. Review exercises. Boring films. I'd gotten hold of a program of your trip. I went to the school library, the multimedia library, too. I borrowed books about monuments in London. The museums you were visiting. That's how I came upon the Hockney painting you don't remember."

"I don't know what to say, Alexandre."

"Then don't say anything, Louis. And let me suck the blood out of your soul. It will be my revenge and my tribute. Would you like a beer?"

"Is it going to feature in the painting?"

The gentle irony in his smile. A knowing wink. He murmurs that the series of portraits he's begun, with the one of his parents, has come at just the right moment. It is forcing him to take stock for the first time. To find out what matters. To see what he can off-load. He murmurs that he doesn't know how well I can understand him, but he feels that I, too, am available now. Unoccupied, in any case. A letting-go in the attitude I've been adopting during the sittings. A rare quality of absence.

"As if you were wandering off somewhere, and that's all that interests me, in other people. This vagabonding. Your mind tramping through the countryside, hesitating whether or not to get completely lost. Especially when, as is the case with you, or me, everything is hidden beneath a thick layer of normality and placidity."

"Sometimes you give me a shiver right down my spine."

Alexandre crushes his cigarette against the metal railing and with a flick that is a touch too theatrical sends the butt flying down onto the grass below. He smiles and replies that this probably explains why he doesn't share his life with anyone and never has, for any length of time. No one likes feeling icy shivers down their spine all the time.

I am walking through the London streets. The light is fading, even though it is only three o'clock in the afternoon. February is already ready to turn nocturnal. In the lining of my leather jacket I have my train ticket and my passport. I touch them at regular intervals. I would like to think things over. To think clearly. Weigh the possibilities, and make clear decisions. I can't seem to manage. My thoughts freeze the moment they break through the layer of ice in my brain. At night my sweat, too, is icy.

I came to spend a few days here to try to give direction and meaning to the life I am leading, and events unraveled so quickly that I am more confused than ever, now. I have been staying in north Camden, in Samuel's apartment. He left France almost five years ago now, doing one odd job after another, stockpiling experience, and, gradually, he has found his way. At a party one night he met Peter, thirty-three years old, a senior executive at an import-export firm who wanted a change of career, to start his own business. The 1980s were nearly over, but the Berlin Wall was still standing and the Enemy was still in the East. Peter explained to whoever would listen that this was the time, now or never, to become an entrepreneur. He'd come up with an enticing plan, a fast food restaurant chain that would use fresh quality produce primarily from local suppliers. Sandwiches. Salads. Meals that could be quickly reheated. The opposite of the fast-food joints saturating the market. The prices would be higher than the competition, but would reassure customers as to the upmarket side of what they were consuming. The clientele, according to Peter, was there waiting. All those young university graduates who no longer had time to go out for lunch and who were sick to death of white bread with cucumber and cream cheese, or greasy hot dogs, hamburgers, and fish and chips. Peter's enthusiasm was contagious. He had managed to sweet-talk the banks and the investors. Samuel could not resist his charm, either. In no time they had become partners, both business and sexual. They knew the situation might be tricky, but they were barely in their thirties yet, and the world was their oyster. Still, Samuel insisted on keeping the studio he'd been renting before he met Peter. Just in case. So I moved in, temporarily.

I had run into Samuel during Christmas vacation, in France. He had come back to see his parents for the holidays. He was wandering around the pedestrian streets of this town he'd grown up in, wondering how he'd managed to stay there for so long. We stopped and said hello. Samuel and I are childhood friends. Our parents were neighbors when we were in primary school so we used to walk to school together. We sat at the same desk all through elementary school. In those days we knew each other inside out. Our passions (comic books and soccer figurines for him, planets and the RTL radio hit parade for me), our fears (ending up naked in the courtyard for him; losing all my family members at one blow for me), our moments of doubt, our aching heads, stomachs, souls. On days off we used to go to the vacant lot behind the redbrick apartment building. We met up with the gang of boys and girls who lived in the neighborhood. We tried to build cabins. We told lies. Boasted. Then Samuel's parents moved a few miles away and enrolled him in a different collège. *At that age, it's enough to destroy all the fragile bridges you've built. We saw each other again briefly at the* lycée, *but it was a huge place; we weren't taking the same courses, and we had nothing to say to each other anymore. I don't know what drew me toward him on that late December day. Or actually, I do. It was what I had heard about him, through a mutual friend, one night at a bar. I admired the way his life was unfolding. Mine was so much more low-key. I was teaching English, surrounded by other teachers, some of whom had been my own teachers. I should have been satisfied, but I was going through a rough patch. At the age of twenty-eight I was still single, whereas all my acquaintances were getting married and starting families.*

By the way, I said to Samuel that day, I've decided to go to London on my own, this time, during the February break. So I can take stock. Get some distance, as people say. I stifled a guffaw which spoke volumes about how embarrassed I felt. Samuel immediately offered to let me use his flat, since he stayed there only very rarely now. He also invited me to meet his friends. To go with him to parties. To immerse myself in his life, since I thought it was so much more brilliant than my own. It's a rare thing, to have someone open the door for you onto a completely different life. I rushed right in, for almost two weeks.

One night in the kitchen of a loft near Swiss Cottage I shared a joint with Jane, who had just become head of a group of shops near Camden specializing in secondhand clothing. It was a growth market. She was looking for a partner. Was I interested? I burst out laughing. I replied that I had no experience in the field. She shrugged and said that I was French, that the town I came from was well known for its factory outlets, that I seemed the levelheaded sort, I wouldn't be obsessed with marketing strategies, but I would be sensitive all the while to innovation, and that I managed fine in English. That was enough. For the rest, I could learn as I went along. She added that she might be stoned at the moment, but she was in earnest. To be honest, she did already have an ideal candidate for the job, but he'd knifed her in the back in the past and she would rather tell him to get lost. The pill would be easier to swallow if he found out he'd been replaced by a Frenchman, a stranger to their circle. I smiled. I gave her the number where she could reach me, at Samuel's flat, but of course she already had it. I added that I would wait for her call before I gave her offer any serious consideration. She called the next evening. She wanted to see me. I'd charmed her. And Peter and Samuel's example was proof that Franco-British relations had good times in store, both sexually and professionally. It was Sunday, February 21. I had one week of vacation left.

We met again. We listened to each other. Breathed. Got undressed. Since then, I've been walking through the city. Trying to tame the capital. What surprises me most is that I can easily imagine living here. All these streets I wander down:

they will soon become the setting for my life. Mentally I draft the letter I'll write to the school administration. Over and over I think: "As I have found a better-paid position in the country whose language I have been teaching, I am writing to inform you that I am handing in my resignation." It is my mantra. My magic formula for an unexpected existence. Of course, I'll miss my friends but over time our relations have become more tenuous, particularly now that they are all sailing off into the calmer waters of a longed-for family life. I am not sure I have any wish to follow them.

Unintentionally, I find myself near Chinatown. I remember a novel I read back in the early 1980s. It was called Adrift in Soho. *The cover of the paperback showed a dark-haired young man with a determined air walking past an English bookshop. An almost-vagabond. An almost-me. I'd like to stop this flow of contradictory thoughts and feelings washing over me. I hope that one day I will think back on this period and smile. An anecdote, along life's way. A decisive turning point. Or a glitch. I'm eager for that moment.*

Next Sunday I'll go back to France to get ready to leave for London for good. One week later, having put all my inhibitions and my characteristic awkwardness behind me, I will go up to Anne during a party in honor of my imminent exile. Everything will suddenly be called into question. I will never hear from Jane again. She doesn't know it, but she has given her middle name to my youngest daughter. And on the far side of the Channel there is the faint dotted outline of the life I could have led, going along its way. I will die a haunted man.

THE END OF NOVEMBER. We are side by side again. Not speaking. I can hear his deep breathing, and mine, more uneven. Our gazes converge on the canvas.

First of all, the verdigris. A color I have always associated with the Second World War, my father's tales of exodus, how at the age of ten he had to cross part of France to reach a zone that would be safer than the flatlands in Lorraine where he lived. With planes flying overhead. The fear. The hunger.

Then the vermilion, emphasizing the bridge of the nose and the curve of the brow. I am a tired warrior. I sat down on that chair when I should have been squatting, my buttocks on my heels, on the lookout. Except that my body is sagging, and I'm no longer as alert as I once was. And there was this chair lying around in the bush for me. I hesitated before sitting on it. I was afraid it was a trap. Opposite me was this other hunter. Far more subtle. A healer, no doubt. He motioned to me to sit. Now it is his strange charm that has taken effect. I'm not sure I want to get back up.

The mauve—incongruous, along the jawbones. An almost feminine touch that is contradicted by the orangey

yellow of the pupils. A reminder of the first layer. The gene-
sis. I am a monster. A hero. My head is spinning. Alexandre
clears his throat.

"I . . . I think I've finished."

I nod. We stand there motionless. We both know we
don't want to part. We are searching for incantatory formu-
las. We can't find any.

"I thought that . . . Well, I had already mentioned it
but . . . it's like with my parents . . . I can't envisage this painting all by itself."

I acquiesce. I ask how many. Alexandre flushes bright red
and walks away. Past the bar. Stops to make a coffee. Belches
a reply. "Three." Adds that before he finds out whether I will
give my consent or not, I need to speak to him. About the
portrait. My impressions. It's hard, of course. But it's important to him, absolutely vital, decisive, because he can easily
muddle everything with black paint, or burn the whole
thing, not a problem, it wouldn't be the first time; you have
to give things a try, screw up, that's how you find what you're
looking for.

"I didn't realize I was so wild, Alexandre."

He shakes his head. He adds that he had noticed right
away, the night of the opening. He had been talking with
some friends-colleagues-rivals, sometimes you can scarcely
tell the difference anymore, and I came into the main room,
frowning, with a half smile that was almost carnivorous.
He had watched from a distance as I wandered around the
rooms. He suddenly noticed how his heart beat faster when

my expression was appreciative, or how he felt pangs of humiliation when I stood with indifference in front of some of the paintings. He realized I was one of the only people—along with his parents, probably—who did not belong to the art world, and whose opinion mattered to him. He wished it were not so. He would have liked to be free of the judgment of those who brought him into the world and those who meant something to him. He remembered me as someone whose ironical kindness stunned him, whose inflections eased tension—but that night he discovered a raw side that destabilized him and snagged him, yes, like a fish on a hook.

"I think that over the years you've constructed an idealized portrait of who I am, Alexandre. It happens sometimes, with people you see from time to time but don't really know. The confrontation with reality is often disappointing. And liberating. I don't like being put on a pedestal. I feel uncomfortable. All I want is to blend into the crowd. Just the opposite from you, right? I am touched by what you've said, but I don't deserve all that praise. You've created your own fiction."

"I know. And I'm confronted with it as I paint you."

"This might be tough to hear, but to be honest, I've never had even the faintest notion of how much I might matter to you. So much the better, actually, because I'm sure I would have panicked and backed out. I would have re-created distance. The little chunk of mental ice floe that should always separate students from teachers. Because we aren't there to be liked. We are there to give, to share, and to guide. That's something very different."

"You were my ray of sunlight, Louis."

I would like to answer, say something evasive to sidestep this past intimacy being unveiled to me, but I can't find the right words. I'm disarmed. Alexandre has turned his head to one side. He is staring at the portrait again. He talks to this image of me that is observing him in return. He sighs. He tells me how he used to come to the lycée feeling sick at heart. A new day about to vanish. One body among others. Often shoved here and there. Not aggressively. Simply because he didn't really exist. And back at home, his parents' reproving silence: ever since he had reached puberty they'd been watching him suspiciously. There was something wrong. He isn't the son everyone praised. He's strange. Disappointing. He spends his time letting us down. So, when he came to my classroom, for a few minutes or sometimes for the whole hour, he was somewhere else. The language we spoke there. The peals of laughter. A kindness. "Even Larmée didn't act out as much, once you had put him in his place, Louis. It was my breathing space. Three hours a week. Sometimes it was enough to keep me going." His struggle was to keep going. In his diary he ticked off the number of weeks he'd managed to hold out so far. He was proud of himself. No one suspected how heroic he felt.

"That's what I'm trying to convey, Louis. The spark."

His laughter rings false. He clenches his fists and lightly strokes the bump on his left hand. On his face, a brief, intense passage of pain. His jaws contract. He purses his lips. Grits his teeth. Relaxes imperceptibly. The hardest is behind him. I kick the ball into play.

"Three paintings, then."

"A triptych, yes."

"Variations for the second one?"

"I'd like to go deeper. I . . ."

His words hang in midair for a few seconds. And again that blushing, rising from his chest but going no farther than his neck.

"Could you . . . um, I'd like you to pose bare-chested."

Words flying between us. Dead leaves drifting to the ground. "Like Lucian Freud?" He looks down. Murmurs that he wouldn't go so far as to compare himself to Freud, of course, but that he is trying to paint in that spirit, now. Rawness and kindness together. A challenge. He adds that, obviously, he'd understand perfectly well if I took him for a lunatic and wanted to put an end to our collaboration. He'd be devastated, but he doesn't want to force anything on me, and anyway, he doesn't have that power; what a stupid conversation, as we've been talking he has realized how ridiculous it is, isn't it, honestly, the whole thing doesn't make sense, "Forget it, Louis, honestly, forget it."

I unbutton my shirt. Painstakingly. I know my body by heart. I'm not particularly proud of it. I'm hairy, and almost uniformly pale. I didn't look after my abs the way I should. A bulging midriff that means a misshapen build. My skin is calloused in places, almost baby-like in others. Still bearing the marks of multiple surgeries. Not long before my divorce I had one skin infection after the other: huge boils, carbuncles—I was rotting from within. What remains are the epidermal inscriptions of a bygone era. I'm a pathetic gladiator.

My blue-and-white shirt is lying at my feet. I lean back into the green armchair Alexandre brought up from the living room. I lift my head and feel an insolence in my eyes when I meet Alexandre's gaze. He stands motionless. On the lookout. Studying the ensemble, then the detail, the grain of my skin, the sheen on the surface, the tense smile of scars. His breathing becomes more sustained, more audible.

"Good."

His word snaps in the air in the apartment. One minute more and he moves away. His entire figure becomes softer, droops. He is back amid his failings, his hesitancy. He asks me if I'm cold. If I want him to turn up the heat. I shrug. I'm half naked under a glass roof. I can't figure out whether I'm in the midst of a dream or a nightmare. He takes his sketchbook and his charcoals. He says we'll take a break in an hour or an hour and a half. He doesn't ask for my consent.

RAW UMBER

"I CAME TO SEE HOW YOU'RE DOING."

Anne removes her scarf and runs her hand through her hair. Sleet has been falling intermittently since dawn. November is fraying with icy little steps. I work out how long it's been since I've seen my ex-wife. Three months, I think. The last time, she was on her way to the swimming pool. I found her radiant. She looks a bit more rumpled this morning, but she is still magnificent. I have to say it—straight out and without any misplaced flattery, and despite what some of my colleagues think: I believe I have truly finished mourning our relationship. We parted on good terms, much to our daughters' displeasure, for they would have liked screaming and bawling and tears. The time for that had passed. We had depleted desire by raising children and we'd reached a point where we were chipping away at the tenderness we felt for each other. We thought it was better to break up before we felt hatred, or scorn. We are grateful to each other for that. After she left I had no sexual relations for almost two years, and when the opportunity came along, I was probably a disappointing lover. In any case, one thing is for sure: I can't imagine falling in love again, the very phrase seems out-moded and inadequate. I've been going around in a sort of equanimity, with brief pauses for the occasional casual affair. I live alone. I'm not proud of it, but I have to confess that it is a lot more bearable than I would have thought. Anne, on the other hand, has started a new life with Gauthier, even though she hates the expression. I occasionally invited them over for a drink on a Sunday evening, once the girls had left for their respective places of study. She would never admit it, but she can't stop looking at him, and despite the slight disquiet brought on by an untimely remnant of jealousy, I am glad for her. He's a calm, thoughtful man, full of humor.

"That's sweet of you. I'm sorry I didn't answer your last message."

"Can you make me a coffee?"

"I warn you, it will take awhile. I haven't cleaned the coffeemaker in ages."

"You're still anticapsule?"

"You know me."

"Well, do I, that's what I've been wondering."

"I beg your pardon?"

"Look, I won't beat around the bush. I've been hearing rumors, Louis."

"By Jove! About me?"

"Stop it, please. You've been seen with Alexandre Laudin, more than once."

"I would love to know the identity of the elusive person who is the agent in this passive sentence."

She gives an irritated wave of the hand.

"Several people. It's a small town. You know that as well as I do."

"Let's just say I'm surprised you care about gossip. And that people have been coming to tattle to you about my goings-on, even though we've been apart for a long time."

"You are still the father of my children. I expect that is of some importance. But that's not what we're talking about."

"What we're talking about is, is my ex-husband having it off with a cool young dude."

She raises her hand, is about to reply, thinks better of it, sighs, then gives a faint smile. She asks if she can sit down. She would like to drink that coffee I promised her, too. She is tired, and thinks I'm failing the most basic requirements of hospitality. I mumble an excuse. Anne has always been good at causing me to stutter and mumble. When we were first together, I had trouble starting my sentences. I kept telling myself she was far too good for me and I didn't have a hope in hell. Deep down I haven't really changed my opinion. I think she wasted part of her life, being with me. One of those discreet disasters, even when everyone else thinks you're the very image of the perfect couple, because only the party most concerned can understand the extent of the disaster. She should have been with someone who would magnify her. Deify her. Elevate her. I was not of that caliber. Whatever the case, I'm always glad to see her. And our daughters are the proof that, on average, we still managed to pull off a few of our projects.

The coffeemaker spits out a brownish liquid which Anne

stares at with faint disgust. She says she shouldn't have come. She knew it. She is ridiculous. Of course I'm right. Both of us are free to do what we like. She explains that she was worried, is all. It's my turn to smile.

"The girls are worried because I don't go out enough and you're worried because suddenly I have a social life," I say.

"No. No, no. I am really glad you're seeing people again. And you can come and have dinner with us whenever you like. It's just that... Alexandre Laudin, honestly! I don't see what you could possibly have in common with him."

"He's a former student, for a start."

"Yes, I remember."

"What? That would surprise me, because I can hardly remember him being in my class at all."

"I'll explain. What are you doing with him?"

"You want to know if we're sleeping together? Maybe you're jealous?"

The look she shoots me wants to be full of scorn, but only manages to express the tenderness she still feels for me. This touches me more than I would have expected. And probably more than it ought to.

"He's an artist, Anne."

"Thanks, I know."

"So he's painting my portrait."

The words float up toward the kitchen ceiling, then drift gently downward in silence, snowflakes melting on the table, leaving a trace of moisture between us. The sound of a car horn farther down the street. A stream of insults. Tires squealing. Someone almost had an accident. Anne gently shakes her head, murmurs that it's worse than she thought. Adds that I've become a muse now. And suddenly her deep laughter. Not a trace of bitterness or irony. She apologizes, says she doesn't know what came over her, it's so stupid, no, not stupid, unexpected, no, not really that unexpected, when you think about it. She would like to know whether I had felt any predisposition in him. The artist he would become. I shrug. I reply that in fact I don't really remember what he was like as a student. He made drawings, yes, but everyone draws at that age, don't they? Like everyone, I kept up with his career in the press, but I have to confess that I'd been surprised by the scope of it. He had never been one of those kids who stood out or whose every move you remember years later.

"The reverse isn't true, however."

"Thirty-five kids in a class and only one teacher. Obviously, they remember us, and sometimes they're hurt because their name no longer means a thing to us."

"He came to the house."

"He what?"

"I can still see his face. He was looking for you. He was nervous. He wanted to hand in some homework. Optional, apparently. He got muddled, trying to explain. Pauline came down to see what was going on. Her being there made him even more embarrassed. I thought he might be in love with her. It was a Wednesday. You had just left to take Iris to her drama lesson."

"You never mentioned it."

She smiles. She explains that he made her promise not to tell me. He was ashamed of what he'd done; he knew very well that he had no right to go and see a teacher on his day off. He was terribly sorry he'd come. He would hand in the homework the next day. He was sorry. Sorry. Sorry. "He seemed to be in such a panic that I took pity on him. I agreed not to mention his visit. I thought I'd ask you later how the matter ended and then I forgot. It's funny. I recalled that episode a few years ago, when I saw his picture for the first time in the newspaper, but at the time we had so many other fish to fry." She breaks off for a few seconds. Mumbles that she hopes that. Stops. No, nothing. I touch her hand. Assure her that she can speak openly to me now that our paths have diverged.

"I'm the mother of your children, after all."

"They're grown up. They've left home. Gone."

She pouts briefly. Plays with the little finger of her right hand. A gesture she's always made.

"You're not doing anything . . . well . . . reprehensible, are you? That could hurt the girls' reputation? No, don't answer. I hear my own words and I cannot believe what I am saying. I am pathetic."

"You've never been pathetic. Listen, it's a painting, Anne. Not a skin flick. And anyway, I'm not naked. Besides, who will even care, huh, honestly? I don't think the paintings will ever even be shown some day. It's a very personal project of his, or so I've understood. He's already done a painting of his parents, but no one has the right to see it."

86

I see my shirt on the floor again. I hear Alexandre murmuring, "Yes. Good." I've told a half-lie. I'm opening up only so far to the woman who was my other half. The thought makes me smile. Anne seems offended. She thinks I'm making fun of her. I dodge the subject. It's easy. All I have to do is mention Iris. Canada. Distance. In no time we are back on the freeway of conversation between divorced parents. We have left the troubled waters of intimacy behind. Before leaving she does, however, go back there, a fleeting touch. She says she was very happy to see me again, that we've let too much time go by, that we have to fix a date for dinner, with Gauthier. All the phrases you feel obliged to say in order to give a little sparkle to your farewell. We are standing together in the doorway. She will soon be swallowed by the darkness. She places her hand on my cheek. I kiss her palm. I notice when I go back into the kitchen that we didn't even drink our coffee. The cups, spoons, and pack of sugar are there, pointless. They would make a magnificent still life.

She turns the key in the ignition. The throb of the engine. She doesn't pull out of the parking space right away. She glances around, turns her head, gives me a last wave with a smile. What is contained in our gaze: a compressed album of the last quarter century that has just gone by. An imperceptible movement of her shoulders, as if she were adjusting a shawl that was about to slip off, then she releases the hand brake and pulls out into the street. A few seconds and she is already gone. I stand there motionless on the sidewalk, my arms dangling. I follow her with my gaze. As far as the intersection of Rue de la Visitation. I narrow my eyes. Then on to the Avenue du Général-Leclerc. And yet I have always sworn I would never behave this way. Like a beggar. A sparrow on a balcony on a winter day, asking for its pittance. I hate myself, but I can't help it.

Her car has stopped at the red light at the end of our street. My street, I mean. I can picture her, nervous, her foot on the accelerator. Frowning slightly. She is trying to avoid the rear-view mirror. She can't. She can see my tiny form. She curses quietly while tears moisten her lashes. She murmurs that there's nothing she can do, after all, is there? That's life. Parents get old, children go their way, everything is as it should be. She hears the Jeanne Moreau song that her mother used to hum to put her to sleep. Des bagues à chaque doigt ... des tas de bracelets autour des poignets. *She clenches her teeth. Gets a grip. She knows that if she goes on like this she'll be overwhelmed, and what's the use of that. She thinks the traffic light is endless. She's getting impatient. She would like me to disappear, now.*

She concentrates on what's next. The two hundred kilometers of autoroute *she will devour in an hour and a half. The late afternoon listening to the radio and the Info Trafic news flashes. The Sunday evening blues she will try to banish by turning the volume up full blast. Then there will be Cyril—he, too, will be on his way back from a weekend with family. From time to time they will share this experience. They know their parents are glad to see their children on their own now and again. Like before. They will exchange their impressions over the ever-present lemon sponge cake that Cyril's mother has baked. They will fill the freezer with all the meals she concocted for them. They will shake their heads and mutter, "Oh, honestly," but they'll be glad all the same. They will smile. Cyril will ask: "What about you? Your mother? And how's your dad?"*

Later on that evening she will do some quick mental arithmetic, something she has gotten used to, then she'll go on the Internet and, caught in the Web, contact her younger sister. She'll tell her in detail about her weekend, exaggerating the boring sides of weekends in the provinces, the perpetual Saturday evening pizzeria, the traditional stroll along the Vienne riverbank on Sunday morning. Iris will laugh wholeheartedly.

She will tell her sister that she is really very brave to put herself through all that. Pauline will give a shrug. A cloud will pass by the window. Memories of marching up and down the stairs, games of hide-and-seek, half-finished drawings, chocolate cake for rainy afternoons. It's all in the distant past, now. Iris will bring her sister back to reality. She will ask for news of me. Pauline will reply that I am looking better, really. She will add that she won't worry as long as I'm still active, particularly since I'm teaching, and I'm in contact with teenagers every day; of course it's exhausting, but at the same time it helps keep me on my toes and in touch with the world, doesn't it? Iris will ask whether I mentioned their mother. She still dreams of children's fairy tales where after countless ordeals the prince and the princess find each other, and even though they are too old now to have any more children, still live happily ever together and look after their grandchildren. Pauline will retort that no, not once, but that she thinks on the whole it's a good sign, it means I'm not stuck in that bygone era, "What would be good, now, would be for him to meet someone, don't you think, Iris? When I see Mom with Gauthier . . . "

A brief pause. Two sighs. One on either side of the screen. They will be completely reassured only the day they know I am with someone again. Someone by my side to listen with a smile when I grumble. To make sure I'm eating properly. Mentally, my daughters see me as two decades older than I actually am.

A brief pause. The light turns green. Two sighs. One inside the car and the other, mine, when she turns onto the Avenue du Général-Leclerc and I lose sight of her. I stand there useless on the sidewalk. I can't bring myself to go back inside. I figure that as long as I am out here, part of her is still close to me. And with her, the ghosts of her sister, her mother, and the family we made, at a certain point in time. It's Sunday evening. There are thousands of us like this, aging adults, standing motionless outside the door to a building or the gate to a house, trying to reconstruct an afterward, while the moles of the present are digging tunnels through our memory.

A WEEK GOES BY. Then two. Alexandre had warned me that he'd be out of town, meeting with gallery owners in Amsterdam. He'd be gone for three or four days. He would get in touch when he got back so that we could continue our sessions of pictorial scalpel. I am beginning to worry. I leave a message on his landline. On his cell. I hate it when I behave like this. I feel like some jilted mistress begging for attention. I wish I could be more detached. Almost otherworldly. I don't want to have anything more to do with emotional dependency—be it with friends or lovers. Advancing age—normally—helps to create this sort of distance.

My profession has come to the rescue, as always. I am working on new course material. I pare down my lesson plans to get right to the essentials. In class, my attitude has changed as well. I have regained that ideal of flexibility and firmness we all strive for. The students are surprised. They look up. Narrow their eyes. Sit up straight. They murmur, too, in the corridors. What has gotten into him? He's weird. Better? No idea. Different, in any case. It's as if he decided to take things in hand again.

While I'm at the lycée, Alexandre Laudin and the first portrait fade, leaving behind nothing but an unpleasant impression. It's a familiar feeling. After my divorce I had a brief period of intense professional activity. I immersed myself in work. My colleagues reproached me for my Stakhanovism. I wouldn't hold up at that tempo, they said. They were right. Along came the first vacation, and everything fell apart. I slid slowly down a slope of clay, toward the bottom of a well where I felt safe, because I was no longer obliged to watch the world hurtling by. Eventually I grew numb. I felt cozy in that environment even if it was unwholesome, but at least it had the merit of reassuring me.

Ten, twenty times I pick up my cell phone, about to send a smooth or provocative message. I recall my adolescence. When I was sixteen or seventeen, I couldn't live without my friends. I was with them all day long and I missed them the moment I left them. I would spend the evening in the phone booth across the street from my parents' house. I'd perfected a system so I wouldn't have to pay for my calls. A five-franc coin attached to a thread that I pulled taut the moment the call went through. I'd go home red in the face, my throat dry. My mother worried about my mental health. She said it wasn't good for me to be that dependent on a circle of friends. "You make your way through life on your own, Louis, alone, whether you like it or not. Others can help you or make your life better, but they don't find your way for you." I didn't want to believe her. When I turned thirty I began to doubt. I swallowed every lie, every friend's betrayal without flinching.

I focused on family: my wife, my daughters. Then they left, too. I abdicated. I was about to concede that my mother had been right—I was stuck in a rut of my own creating. Until the exhibition. As I gazed at Alexandre Laudin's crowds, those garish, anguished faces, part of me rebelled. I believe fundamentally in others. In the good they do us in spite of all their failings. In the colors they give us. The portraits they paint of us.

I called a few colleagues whose integrity and humor I have come to appreciate over all our years of shared vocation. I suggested a dinner. At my place. Charles accepted my invitation, referring ironically to how I'd been talking about it for ages without ever getting around to it. The other two simply took note and added they were delighted, they could bring their spouses, couldn't they, we wouldn't be talking about work?

It's Saturday evening. Fourteen days since my shirt ended up on Laudin's living room floor. Soon it will be no more than a bad memory. One of those things burned into memory that forces you to lower your eyes when the images catch up with you in the bathroom mirror. My colleagues are discussing the situation in the country. Rampant racism. The rise of extremism. I listen. I nod my head. I pour more wine. The remains of the meal are spread before us. Outside, the clouds are tinged with yellow. It will probably snow before long. A trembling against my left thigh. A quick look. A text message from Laudin. He'd like to see me, as soon as possible. This evening? I switch the cell phone off. He can wait.

"I TRIED SEVERAL TIMES TO REACH YOU, LOUIS."

"I couldn't be reached, Alexandre."

"Something wrong?"

"Not at all. Life. Meetings. Work. Busy-busy."

I'm back in the green armchair. I've resumed my pose. I didn't need to work at it. My memory had incorporated it. Legs spread. Hands on thighs. Torso sagging slightly. Lips tightly pressed. And insurrection in my gaze—I didn't have to go looking for that, either. It was there, lying in wait, ready to attack.

"I really wanted to work on this painting some more. It has been obsessing me, for days on end. I think I couldn't let go of your skin."

Alexandre lets out a grating little laugh that isn't like him. He coughs twice. He looks exhausted. All those trips. All those parties. I'm not going to feel sorry for him. Then, silence. Slowly, intimacy returns. Treading stealthily. Sensing the obstacles that come of eighteen days of not seeing, brushing past, or sensing each other. We are having trouble settling back into our lair.

"You're awfully quiet, Louis. Would you rather we didn't speak?"

We look at each other and for the first time our gazes linger. What I can see troubles me. Behind the vacillating light there is a sense of renunciation.

"Why did you wait so long to get back in touch?"

The faint rubbing of brush on canvas. I don't move an inch.

"Did you miss me?"

"I hate this sort of lovers' game you're playing."

"So you did miss me. Unless it was your own self you didn't want to be around again. This image of yourself. Passive, while I'm painting your portrait."

"I was convinced I wouldn't be coming to pose anymore."

"And I was convinced I'd be giving up the project."

"Really?"

"Absolutely."

My point of view shifts, for the first time since the beginning of this adventure. I had never imagined the scene as viewed from the easel. What Laudin might be feeling. How it was affecting the course of his existence. I answer that I would have understood perfectly if he'd decided not to go on. He wouldn't even have had to give me any explanation. It is disturbing, this closeness to a figure from the past, after all. Someone whose shape is familiar but about whom you really know nothing, in the end. I add that he could simply have let me know. Even just about his doubts. It would have been more polite. More civil. I am sounding like a teacher in front of a student who has skipped a test and is trying to wriggle out of it. Laudin smiles, but his smile doesn't rekindle a flame in his eyes.

"I'm sick, Louis."

I instantly see hospital corridors, flashing ambulance lights, overcrowded waiting rooms. I drop my arrogant stance. I nod, mutter apologies. Alexandre replies that it's no problem, it's nothing to do with me. Or rather, it is, on second thought, but not in the way I might suppose. The series of paintings probably stems from the diagnosis. Like the desire to turn everything upside down. And attack, clear down to the bone. He adds that I mustn't worry, he's not about to die any time soon, or probably not even in the decade to come; it's a slow-dissolving pill he's had to swallow. I frown. His tone turns flat. A recital he's learned by heart, to stay as neutral as possible and prevent any outpourings of compassion. The pain started four years ago, he explains, but in the beginning, obviously, he didn't pay any attention. His hands. His back. All perfectly normal for someone who spends hours at an easel. He signed up for yoga. Went to see a physiotherapist. Joked and said he'd always looked old for his age. There was this lump that appeared, swelled, then shrank again, at the joint between his index and middle finger on his left hand. He realized he had a tendency to hide it in the presence of others. He dreaded their questions. Sometimes he woke up during the night and his heart was beating faster, but he couldn't bring himself to go to a doctor. He had this stupid notion that if he saw a doctor it would make him sick rather than making things better. Then one day he was in a *parfumerie* in Paris; he loved going into those galleries filled with scents, they inspired him. He had chosen a fragrance for men, was holding the bottle between his fingers, and suddenly a searing pain rose from his wrist and radiated all the way through his bones to his fingertips . . . He dropped the bottle and it shattered on the floor, to the stunned silence of the customers, who didn't even notice or care about the shards of glass, so distraught were they at the sight of his pain-distorted face. They called the emergency services, even though he didn't want that, and kept saying the crisis was over, it was nothing. Later, he went to a specialist. He remembers how after every sentence he uttered the man would nod. And the words the doctor wrapped around the patient, to accompany him and invite him gently to come and gaze at the extent of the disaster. Rheumatoid arthritis. Two *h*'s and three *t*'s. Dry letters marking out an extremely solitary space. A disease that most of the population suffers from by the time they reach advanced old age. Joints attacked. Deformed. Ravaged. We can all remember an old aunt with her hands curled in on themselves, unable to pick up the most ordinary object.

"You see, I'm that old aunt. Half a century early."

I get up. Put on the shirt I'd left on the floor. I can hear the crinkling of plastic beneath my feet—a drop cloth will be needed here for some time. Alexandre frowns and his eyes start to flash. He grumbles that he hates displays of empathy. That it's very embarrassing. And I have better things to do than come and express my old man's solidarity with someone twenty years my junior. I don't listen to a thing he's saying. In a corner of my memory he has just reemerged, intact. His fugitive gaze. The way he would press back his cuticles with his nails. His insistence on staring at the wall in front of him, as if the wall were about to open suddenly and reveal the mysteries of the universe to him. Alexandre Laudin. Sixteen years old. That is who I want to hold in my arms, to comfort. Everything will be fine, Alexandre. You have a future. And it is bright. Shining. Rounded. Full.

He struggles for a few seconds, murmuring, "Go away," and then suddenly the dikes break. I think of my daughters. Of the fear that suddenly came over them when they tried to imagine the future.

By the time I sit back down, the quality of the air has changed. The aggressive atmosphere has vanished. All that remains is this strange empathy between us, still somewhat formal. Alexandre concentrates on his paint. Brown, above all, he said, confidentially. It's a color he uses often, but now he is trying new shades. Umber. Raw umber. I smile. I go home. The windows looking out onto the public park. The foliage of trees. I'm back among green. Blue. Yellow. That's where I want to live.

*I'*m lying on the bench by the children's playground. There's a speed bump. A slide. A turnstile. All of it rusty, broken. Orange. Red. Yellow. The benches are a historical relic. White stone, dating from the construction of the velodrome in the nineteenth century. The racing tracks must still exist, underground. Covered over by geological and temporal layers. The velodrome made way for a school, just as the twentieth century was beginning: a complex of brick school buildings, with mosaic friezes on the pediments of each building representing smiling Greek or Roman children on their way to lessons with their masters. No one even notices them anymore, these odd vestiges of an era when teaching was regarded as sacred. No one except me, because I spend hours observing my environment. And seeking oblivion. Yes, that is what I want more than anything, to be forgotten.

I'm eight years old. I am lying on the bench by the playground. I didn't have the courage to climb the chestnut tree. My legs are tucked under me. Passersby on the Rue Édouard-Vaillant can't see me. I'm outside, but protected by the granular stone. And yet even from here I can hear the shouts. The insults. They reverberate in the July air. I figure I'm lucky because almost

100

all the neighbors have gone on vacation. There's no one who will run into me in a few minutes or a few hours. No one will put their hand on my shoulder and murmur, "Everything okay?" as if I had terminal cancer. There won't be any commiseration in people's gazes. Or those words they utter in a hushed voice: "Poor kid, you see, it must be hard on him."

My father is shouting at my mother. That's a fact. An objective given. His invectives and insults spread out into the stairwell, echo from wall to wall, penetrate into the other company apartments, and cause the residents to stop what they're doing, their bodies suddenly tensed. They listen out. They are sure that sooner or later he is going to hit her. For the moment, it's just words, and words aren't the same, words don't bleed, words fly away, like starlings, they create murmurations, they fly in circles and in the end they scatter, as if nothing had happened. "Yes, of course, the boy. Yes, but what could we say, it's not really violence, is it. Long as he's not beating her. Whore, bitch, for sure those aren't very nice words to hear, but hey, who knows, maybe there's some truth in them. And anyway he wouldn't be the first to grow up in an atmosphere of conjugal hatred, look at the number of divorces, always on the rise. I'm sure that deep down something good will come of it. I know, it sounds ridiculous. But you'll see, it will forge his character. After this he'll be able to deal with any situation without being afraid."

Fear is a gentle animal. I feel its fur in the pit of my belly. It began clinging there, half an hour ago, when it all began. For no reason, as usual. A glass not washed properly. A meal too hastily prepared. A phone call from a colleague. I recognized *the omens—I found the word in a novel that wasn't for kids my age, last week, and I looked it up. Now I can identify them, the omens. It's like a shiver running through the apartment—and then, the stillness in the summer heat. Just a few seconds before the storm breaks. When there's no school, or when the neighbors are there, I hide under the bed. I put the little yellow cushions my grandmother gave me over my ears, and I tell myself stories.*

Today is different. The hysteria goes through the open windows and out into the deserted neighborhood. I ran out just before the shouts began. I hurtled down the stairs. I ran over to the playground. I lay on the bench. I can still hear some sounds, but I don't want to block my ears. I want to go on lying here, watching the play of light in the foliage of the willow tree above me. The implacable blue of the sky. The tender green of the leaves. The golden yellow of sunlight. All the nuances. All the alternations—blue, yellow, green, green, yellow, blue. One day I'll learn the names of colors, because once you master the colors, then you can chase the black away.

"I THINK I'M DONE."

Outside, December is gusting. In the garden below, two interjections, a shout, then nothing more. For a few minutes we stay there without moving, both of us. His face is turned toward me, but he is staring into space. I am exhausted, stiff and sore and incapable of stretching. Caught in the spell. Which breaks when Alexandre suddenly stands up straight, on edge, and leaves the room. I stretch my spine. Arch my back. Raise both arms, palms skyward. Find my shirt. Take a few steps. Hesitate. Decide against it. Then yield to temptation.

I stand out against a background of brown edging toward gray. Bright pink. Mauve. Traces of vermilion and golden yellow. The scars that are supposed to repair one's flesh, but only imprison it. Grimacing mouth, chin raised, an expression that is almost concupiscent. I laugh loudly on the edge of a precipice—madness? Death? Wounded, but not martyred. On the border between pleasure and pain.

I feel pride, and immediately afterward I'm overcome with a wave of disgust. A violent urge to retch. I stride quickly across the room, hurry down the stairs, slamming the door behind me. I'm cold. Extremely cold. And this nagging impression that something's missing. Some forgotten accessory—scarf, gloves, bag. A limb, abandoned. No sooner am I out of doors, in the wind again, filling my lungs with air, than Alexandre comes to join me.

"Are you all right, Louis?"

"Look, I need to stretch my legs for a few minutes. Then I'll go home. If you'd like, you can come over. Just give me a little time. Alone."

We meet up early in the evening. Night has already blanketed the town. Alexandre paces back and forth in the apartment before finding his bearings. He points out that you bump into everything here, that it must feel cramped living here, that surely I could find somewhere better. I answer with a smile that he'd do better to come back down to earth and imagine himself in the shoes of a divorced high school teacher, who will soon be getting a fairly modest retirement—"we don't live in the same world, young man." He smiles. He swirls his whiskey in the glass, a whiskey he chose, to my great surprise, from the bar I built and almost never use. He stares into the orange-brown liquid, absorbed.

"Have you seen the painting?"

As soon as he says this the canvas slaps me in the face again. I lean discreetly against the living room table. I nod. I mumble that I don't feel like talking about it just now. Maybe never, actually. It's his work. Not mine. He nods. He pretends to be thinking about what I've said, but his mind is elsewhere. He's in the future. Far ahead of me. He says he's got one remaining, "here"—and points to his left temple. He adds, "You knew that, didn't you?" Then more softly, "Are you okay with that?" I shrug. He explains that he'll be leaving for Vienna soon, and will be there over New Year's. I'm about to reply that I don't need to know his social calendar, that I've already toyed with jealousy and don't like it, when suddenly he invites me to go with him.

"To Vienna?"

"It's a beautiful city. Far less embalmed in the nineteenth century than you might imagine and—"

"I've already been there."

"Really?"

I smile at his surprised expression. I ask him why that seems so strange. Do I look like a man who's never been out of his burrow? If he only knew! In the memory of my retina I have images of Inca fortresses, American parks, and citadels in the desert, even if it is true that it's been a long time since I took a plane. I thought that the next time would be to see my younger daughter, but her life is so busy, and I think she'd rather come back to her hometown and her old ties than welcome her father into her new life. Alexandre mumbles that he just figured Vienna, well, Vienna, after all, it isn't that common a destination, is it?

"Well, it was just that I used to like going around European capitals. But that's another story."

"How old were you?"

"When I was in Vienna? Twenty. It's an odd choice, I

grant you that. Even odder back then, when Austria was a sleepy sort of place."

"You were already with your wife. I mean your ex-wife. Anne, right?"

Without knowing it, he has thrown me a line to help me past awkward memories. I land on the far shore and turn around to look at him. Now I am steering the conversation.

"I saw her recently, by the way. We talked about you. She told me that you had come by the house one day. Back when you were still at the lycée. She had never mentioned your visit before."

Alexandre flushes bright red. He didn't see this coming, didn't have time to prepare himself. He sits down on the red plastic stool in the kitchenette, where I do very little cooking. He opens the drawer in the table, mechanically, takes out a little knife, reaches for an apple and begins to peel it.

"I'm sorry."

"I don't see why."

"For having the nerve to come and ring at the door. For thinking I could barge into your life. It's right near the top of the list of my most embarrassing moments. Your wife was very kind. She spoke to me as if she were dealing with a mental patient. And your daughter was hovering in the background, looking at me and frowning. I'd give anything to be able to go back and break my leg that day. Or erase the images that linger."

"I still don't know why you came."

A sound from his throat—a stifled laugh. Alexandre

shakes his head, his eyes staring at the knife blade, and the apple peel gradually revealing its vegetal nakedness.

"Do you remember *Looking Back*?"

"Do I what?"

"The last composition you gave us that year?"

I make a face. Of course. At the height of my career, I sometimes tried experiments that went beyond the strictly-defined curriculum. With the classes of *première* and *terminale* that were doing well, I would allow myself to slip in a call to introspection for their final written work. "You are forty years old now. You walk past your old school. Images resurface." I'd entitled the exercise "Looking Back." It was optional, but highly recommended, because it would be graded only if it proved to be positive, in light of the fact that my criteria, with this sort of homework, could only be extremely subjective. They were allowed to structure their response in any format they liked—letter, article, essay, comic strip, film. When I read out the topic, I often heard rustling sounds in the classroom—and there were the occasional gestures of defiance, too. I reminded them that they were under no obligation, and above all there were no rules. They couldn't get over it. Almost at once some of them would throw themselves headlong into the project, but give up along the way. Others persevered. In the boxes in my storage room there must still be a few of these clumsy, funny, occasionally touching productions. I never reread them, and yet I have kept them. Now when I think back, this attempt at rendering a foreign language more personal strikes me as interesting but inappropriate. What was I expecting? That they would give me an insight into their private lives? A piece of that youth that was leaving me behind? I sometimes prefer the harmless old fogey I've become to the brilliant but intrusive young teacher I must have been. In any case, I have no recollection of Alexandre Laudin's essay.

He takes a second apple and sets about peeling it as painstakingly as the first one.

"I wrote everything. It was a sort of diary. Shameless. Twenty pages. My life. My work. At the age of seventeen. Pathetic."

He concentrates on the fruit undressing between his fingers.

"On the day the big assignment was due, there was a buzz in the corridors. They all wanted to be the best-looking, the most intelligent, the most noticed. They showed up carrying posters, photomontages, films they'd made with their parents' camcorders, collages, calligrams; it was inventive, sparkling, they were quivering with delight. They wanted to stand out. They wanted to make you cry your eyes out or laugh or blush. It made me sick. I had my twenty pages in my bag, written in awkward English, with words in French penciled in, and my sentences were trying to get to the bottom of what I'd understood upon arriving in that place, which was that, even if everyone claimed to be tolerant, I would never be wholly a part of that huge wave of pretend love. Because I desired my own kind. Boys. And at best that aroused compassion, particularly among the girls, and at worst distrust, and veiled aggression. If only I had accepted the way I was, if I'd known the right way to behave—exuberantly, laughing loudly, always coming up with just the right thing to say—then yes, I would have been allowed into that crowd with their parties, where they made adolescence into one huge carnival. But I wasn't like that. I tried to blend into the background. I nurtured guilt and shame. I wasn't mature enough to realize that my liberation could only come from inside. That I shouldn't expect anything from other people."

Alexandre Laudin clenches his jaw and mutters to himself. He turns the knife blade skillfully. He grabs a third apple. Soon he will have pride of place among the apple peels.

"Were you in love with me, Alexandre?"

The knife pauses for a second. Alexandre shrugs. He says yes of course and no of course not. A fleeting smile. He says that of course I had found my way into some of his erotic dreams, back then, but he was aware of the difference in our ages and status. He also knew that I was married and had children. That there was no hope. Let's just say he'd quickly moved on to something else. And that something else was Matthieu Cintrat.

"You remember Matthieu Cintrat, I'm sure. He was the teacher's pet!"

This last word, exploding; Alexandre's voice, shattered. I give the silence time to settle again. While his breathing grows calmer, I take a chopping board from the cabinet. He starts mechanically slicing the apples and I begin rolling the pastry dough I have just taken from the fridge. Sometimes cooking is all you can go on doing. Finding a shared activity. Avoiding hurtful words. Gazes. Returning safe and sound from that discomfort zone.

Matthieu Cintrat's name is still hovering, but it has lost its sharp edges. I can recall his features easily, but I don't remember treating him as my favorite, particularly—or that he left any impression on me, either. Yes, he was lively, he would get the conversation going again whenever he felt bored, he enjoyed talking in a foreign language—sometimes it was borderline pedantic, so that he could show off the fluency he'd acquired thanks to various stays in English-speaking countries. I think he enrolled in Sciences Po later on, but I lost track of him before long. As I did with so many others.

"To be honest, Alexandre, I have a few images in my mind, but they're very vague."

Alexandre apologizes. He shouldn't have gotten carried away. He really ought to go into therapy. He admits it's really disappointing to have these chunks of adolescence still stuck in his throat. Others seem to have assimilated them no problem. I reply that others, whomever they might be, must dream of having the sort of personal, social, and artistic success that he has. They are bound to read the articles about him, and must feel a certain bitterness, let alone a stab of jealousy—a whole spear's worth. Alexandre relaxes.

"I don't think they do, no. At best, they're annoyed. Or they sneer, remembering the humiliating anecdotes, like the time I got soaked in the boys' restroom because someone had dismantled the faucet."

"You have to stop thinking people have such long memories, Alexandre. Memories fade, or get distorted, but most often they disappear."

"You know what became of Matthieu Cintrat?"

"Not really, no, and I have to confess I don't really care. But I'm sorry if I gave the impression I was more interested in him than in everyone else."

"He got off to a brilliant start at university, then something stopped him. I spoke about it with his parents one day. They came to an opening. They had a favor to ask. Matthieu has been in China for a dozen years or so now. Married, apparently. A father, too. But that was all they knew. He sends them a postcard every year for the new year. A terse message, to say he's still alive. No address or phone number. They wondered whether, with my increasing renown and the networks I'm bound to have created, I could find out anything more. His mother. God. She was old. With this imploring look. This same woman who used to look me up and down on those rare occasions when I ran into her, when I was with Matthieu. I said I'd try. I set all the gears in motion. But I came up empty. He's somewhere in the Middle Kingdom. A needle in a haystack."

"Free."

"Sorry?"

"Haven't you ever dreamed of that? Starting all over, somewhere else? With a different hand, different cards?

Getting lost in the crowd. Anonymous. No more pressure from family or friends. What a relief! If ever you do find him, please don't tell anyone."

"I've given up trying, anyway. I let him live inside me, rather."

Alexandre gently arranges the slices of apple on the dough, as if he were making a mandala. I smile as I watch him. I think of my daughters, the way they used to prepare the batter for their chocolate cake, how they would lick the wooden spoon.

"So you told me all about Matthieu in the pages you brought me that fateful day?"

"Everything. The hell of being in love with someone who can never repay you, because he isn't attracted in the same way. The hell of hanging around the corridors knowing you're transparent, and that you have to consider yourself lucky if no one is giving you a rough time. Just this latent scorn, is all. In short, jeremiads. Self-pity. Everything I despise."

He sighs. When he begins to speak again, his voice is steady, almost mechanical. He had hesitated a long time before coming to my house. Deep down he knew it was a mistake, but a tiny part of him had a blind belief that I would know which way to steer him. Or even care for him. Keep him from suffering. Make him normal. The way I am. With my sunny disposition. The guy who doesn't ask questions and who makes his way through life, and everyone treats him kindly. That was his ideal. That was how he wanted to live. Like me. He wanted to be me. He almost gave up when he reached the top of Avenue du Général-Leclerc. He had never had such painful cramps in his stomach. But he held out. Valiant little soldier. With his pages tucked under his arm, he rang at my door—and reality caught up with him when Anne opened it. And when Pauline crept up behind her, frowning. The ground opened under his feet. He realized there was nothing I could do for him. That he had to continue on his way alone. That was it.

On the floor above, the neighbor has just come home. Her husband has been waiting for her. Snatches of conversation filter through the ceiling. In the kitchen everything is calm. All we hear is the humming of the oven.

"And your love life nowadays, Alexandre?"

He shrugs. He replies that it comes and goes, nothing lasting, a lot of unproductive relationships, just to see if his body is still working and his joints haven't seized up. There were one or two boys—he uses the word "boy"—with whom things might have gone a bit further, but he knows he's not easy to get along with, and his illness doesn't help things. He doesn't want a nurse. He can't stand being dependent. He thinks things might get complicated in the future. He even refuses to think about it. He wants to think about only the near future. He raises his chin and says that, speaking of the near future, I still haven't given him an answer, about Vienna. I say I'll think about it. Between Christmas and New Year's, right? He tells me he's leaving on the twenty-sixth and the gallery owner he's meeting will be lending him a big apartment just off the Ringstrasse, for as long as he likes. Alexandre makes a face: "He has no idea what money is worth," he adds. Alexandre intends to spend New Year's Eve there, and he'd be glad if I came with him, but he is perfectly aware that I might have family obligations.

The Christmas holidays were always a rough period for me, because they reminded me of those New Year's Eve celebrations in my childhood when we never had anyone over and the insults began to fly the moment the smoked salmon was put on the table. Obviously, my perspective changed when my girls were born, but no matter how much Anne and the girls seemed to enjoy these family occasions, I felt like a virtual outsider. I tried to act as if I were having a good time. I think I managed, to a reasonable degree. Since the divorce, it's been another challenge altogether—to remain stoic and smiling, while categorically declining all the invitations from colleagues or vague relatives who worry that you will in all likelihood end up spending the holidays all on your own. Even when you assure them that everything is fine. This year Iris is in Canada and will spend her break with her in-laws, together with Pauline, who is looking forward to spending a few days with her sister.

Alexandre makes clear that of course I don't have to answer right away. I'm not even obliged to answer at all. His flight is on the twenty-sixth; from Paris-Charles de Gaulle; Austrian Airlines at 8:50 a.m.

"I've only been to Vienna once. In the very early eighties. I hated it. Fog everywhere. The Danube Canal all gray and black. The austere facades. And the locals totally uninterested in a cosmopolitan outlook."

"It's changed a lot."

"I guess it has, yes. In any case, it will be a chance to find out."

His smile. For a few seconds he turns his head to one side. Just long enough to ward off the crimson that threatens to redden his skin. Or to hide a grimace of searing pain.

"I DON'T KNOW WHAT I'M DOING HERE."

She's nervous. Glancing from left to right. But no one could possibly recognize us here. We are in one of those chain restaurants on the outskirts of town. This one is supposed to specialize in Italian cuisine, and the food is as insipid as at the surrounding competition: Asian buffets, American grills, Belgian mussels and frites. She's hardly touched her spinach and goat cheese lasagna. As for me, I'm pecking at the Abruzzo salad I ordered as a last resort. I didn't know they produced smoked salmon in Abruzzo.

She sent me a text message at the end of the afternoon. She was just leaving work. She'd been ruminating since our last encounter, she said. She was sorry about the way she'd spoken to me. One message led to another. At one point I wrote that we had to stop this back-and-forth by text because Gauthier would really take umbrage. That was when I found out he was in Lyon on business until the end of the week. I took a deep breath and let a few minutes go by before suggesting I come and see her. Out of the question, she replied. If we are going to meet, it may as well be somewhere neutral.

She suggested this pretentious self-service place at the edge of the town. Now she wonders what got into her.

"If you are afraid of what people might say, or of Gauthier's reaction, make up some excuse. Say that Pauline had a problem and she was in tears when she called you. That you were worried. Remind them at the same time that I'm her father."

"Pauline would probably try to reach Gauthier directly if there was something wrong. I think he may even be first on her list of people to contact in an emergency."

I feel the old sting of jealousy. The one that burned when I found out Anne was seeing someone. I remember above all being afraid I would be replaced in my daughters' hearts. I shouldn't have been surprised, though. Gauthier is a responsible guy, the kind you can count on. There is nothing enviable about his position as stepfather-come-lately, and yet he knew how to turn it into an asset. He belongs to our broken home but he knows how to look at it from the outside, with a neutral yet benevolent gaze. I swallow my acrimony.

"If you think it's a mistake to have come, you can leave when you want. No one is holding you prisoner. Especially not that pile of pasta swimming in béchamel sauce. In fact, is the spinach to ease your conscience?"

She relaxes a little. Smiles faintly.

"Exactly. Actually I hate this dish. I don't know why I ordered it. Or why I'm here. I think I'm a little lost."

"You want us to leave?"

"To go where?"

"For a drive?"

"At ten o'clock at night? In winter?"

"On the bypass?"

"What?"

"We go round and round on the bypass until we run out of gas?"

She is about to offer a retort, then thinks better of it. Pushes her chair back a few inches. Looks up at the ceiling. Agrees. A few minutes later we are in my old car, the heat turned on high. She fiddles with the knobs of the car radio. She's looking for the appropriate music. A station for oldies, with oldies. Refrains we can shout in the car, because sometimes shouting is the only thing you dream of doing.

"*No, but . . . I know when I'm in love.*"

I look up. I try to hide the smile that threatens to spread across my face. She thinks I smile too much, as a rule. That it's suspicious. That I must be the worst sort of hypocrite. Or a nihilist who has decided once and for all that life is a huge hoax. I don't reply. I am hanging on her words. My future depends on her sighs and her silences. Her opening words are gratifying. Maybe we will be able to build something together.

"*But this time, I'm not.*"

For a few seconds I'm like the coyote in the cartoon who has just realized there is no more road under his feet. I press my lips together. I take short breaths, trying to make as little noise as possible. The air burns my sinuses, my nose, my vision. Appearance. That's it. I have to keep up a good appearance. And while my entire being is trying to keep from toppling, disillusion and interrogation collide. But I was convinced that. It was obvious that. When did I make the fatal mistake? And now? Which way do I go? What do I become? Chinks appear in the walls of questions, openings onto the future—narrow, violent visions. I'm twenty-eight years old, almost twenty-nine. I stopped hanging out in discothèques ages ago. I am even beginning to get tired of the bars in the center of town, that rotating gaze I cannot help but give when I go in, because tonight, maybe. All my friends have met the person they will spend their lives with, at least for a few years, the man or woman who will surely be the other parent of their first child. They have boarded their regional express or high speed or local train and I'm the only one still standing on the platform. I wonder what is wrong with me.

Whereas mentally, I am slowly falling, Alice lost in a land of rabbit holes, I picture the months to come. Back in circulation. In bars, in the street, at parties. On the lookout. Exposed. Overexposed. Noticeable. Noticed. Spiritual. But gentle. But virile. But tender. But ambitious. But fragile. But funny. I'm tired. I think I'll give up. I'll become the guy with a bevy of godchildren, who'll refer to him as Uncle Louis when they jump into his arms, while my friends, arms crossed, will watch this touching scene with a smile of commiseration—they will be so glad they chose me as godfather. "Really, it's true, it's so unfair he never found the right woman. He would have been a perfect father. See how much fun he's having with the kids."

I notice my fingers trembling a little as I reach for my wallet. I take a deep breath. I have to calm down. I will nod, as I must. Say that I understand. Of course the problem is her, not me. Yes, yes, yes. A pity, the ball was in her court, but she just lobbed it back in my face. I'll wish her a pleasant evening. Oh, no problem. Of course we'll stay in touch. Friends? That's asking a bit much, don't you think? We don't know each other that well, in the end, do we? But "in touch," sure, absolutely. We have each *other's addresses and phone numbers. Not to worry. I've never worried. I sweep, I take out the garbage, I disappear, I leave no trace. I'm really a great guy. Too bad it never works out.*

I thought I was going to land on a bed of dead leaves and, if need be, find a little golden key that would open the door to Wonderland, but apparently the fall is endless. Somehow I move out-of-body. I watch myself falling. In my eyes there is that resignation I've always despised. That way I submit to the blows of fate, and play Mr. What's-the-Use? The way I dodge the thorny situation by reminding myself that things are a lot worse elsewhere, and whatever happens, a hundred years from now everything will be toast, the climate will be so out of whack that we'll all be fighting to survive, tossing our bonds and beliefs out the window. This refusal to fight.

It is during this endless descent into my private hell that I suddenly realize how much I am going to miss her. Anne. Her stubborn way of taking her life in hand. Her discolored left canine. Her fidgeting fingers. The insecurity she hides beneath an impassive mask. The contact of her skin on mine. My hand around her waist, after lovemaking. I am convinced we would make a delightful duet. Climb to the top of the hill together and run back down, screaming.

And suddenly, bursting out of some innermost hidden recess, rage. Determinism be damned. I am standing up, clumsily leaning forward to present my cheek for the friendly kiss that would feel like a slap, but I say no. No. Quite simply. It cannot be. I sit back down. I see again the images of that film I watched seven times in a row when it came out, and which starts with the funeral of a man who is still young. All his friends gathered there. The eulogies, in the church. The motorcade to the cemetery. All of it to the soundtrack of the Rolling Stones, ringing suddenly like the death knell of a generation. "You can't always get what you want, but if you try sometime, you find you get what you need." That is exactly what I tell her, my eyes deep in hers, my face slightly forward, hesitating between biting and kissing her, fever in my gaze. "I may not be the one you want, but I am sure I'm the one you need. Think about it." When I leave the café I realize that, for what must be the very first time, I have managed to thread my way through the tables without bumping into a single one. Out in the street I clench my teeth. This is the first day of my life alone. Since it didn't work out with her and I'm headed hell-bent for my thirties, I figure it's all not worth the effort. I won't go selling myself to the highest or most desperate bidder. Later, I will write a novel that will begin, "My sex life came to an end when I turned thirty." The readers will laugh at my offbeat tone and the radical humor of my confession. They'll view it as a well-phrased fiction—because, honestly, how can anyone imagine a situation like that lasting any length of time, in our day and age, if the narrator is not a priest (and even then, with everything you hear these days . . .) when in fact it will indeed be an uncompromising statement of fact.

Back in my apartment I sit down on the sofa, holding myself very erect. I don't move. I wait for nightfall. The phone by the armrest rings at around eight thirty. I pick up, force of habit. It's her. She's been going around in circles since she saw me. She keeps thinking about that quotation. She even copied it down on a sheet of paper and pinned it up above her desk. She'd like to know if we can meet again. Fairly soon. This evening, for example, if I don't have anything else planned.

We will spend the better part of twenty years together. We will have two daughters. We will part quietly, without incident. One day, as we are getting dangerously close to our sixties, we will spend part of a night going around and around on the bypass, listening to a radio station devoted to the greatest hits of the previous decades, and we will understand that no matter what happens we are inextricably bound to each other.

SHE WOULD LIKE TO STOP at the next parking lot. She feels like a smoke. I point out that she stopped smoking over ten years ago. She shrugs and says, "So? All the more reason." I tell her she can smoke in the car but she protests—it's out of the question. Afterward the smell lasts for months. I remind her that we did, however, often smoke in the car, before the girls were born. She replies that we also drove drunk and slept with strangers without using a condom. We are not exemplary. She adds, "Hey, just there on the right, by the superstore, that would be fine." I smile. She frowns. She doesn't see what's so funny. I mutter, "Nothing," but I can feel the tear beading at the edge of my eyelashes and I concentrate on the asphalt. I know this penchant she has for end-of-the-world sorts of places—deserted shopping malls, abandoned parking areas on the outskirts of towns, canyons in the American West, jagged ocean shores. She has already admitted that it is there she feels most alive.

Look at us.

The streetlamps on the bypass throw an oblique light on the shopping carts nesting inside one another. We are sitting on the hood. Before us is the mall with its chain stores where we used to get lost with the girls on the occasional Saturday afternoon. She lets the cigarette burn down to her fingertips.

"I'm glad you called, Anne."

"Don't go thinking you're going to ravish me on the backseat."

"I'd never dare. Too afraid I'd throw out my back."

She touches my shoulder, and says, "You know we'll never be a couple again, don't you?"

I nod. I murmur that, to be honest, I think it's a bit sad. She sweeps my words away with a wave of her hand. She tells me she wants to introduce me to someone. Her name is Amélie. She's a bit younger than we are. She is from that generation where it was no longer the fashion to name baby girls Valérie or Véronique or Sylvie or Isabelle. I mumble, "But why, what's the point, really, it's ridiculous, inappropriate." She answers that it's no weirder than acting the muse for a former student who's become an artist. I can't help but laugh. I gaze at her profile, backlit by the neon lights from the gas station a few yards away. We're not that far from the fuel pumps, and we're smoking. The story of our lives, all of us.

"Listen, Anne, honestly...There is nothing...weird about my relationship with Alexandre, I promise you."

"Drop it. I think I'm jealous, that's all."

"I'm not sure I understand."

"You have things happening to you. Events. Encounters. You're asking yourself questions. Feeling your way. It's been so long since chance came knocking at my door. I drive slowly down my back roads, never pass any trucks or motorcycles. I'm caught in a net of everyday chores. I sign up for activities to try and distract myself from the thought that I will soon be retired and I'll have to reassure everyone by saying over and over that I'm a sixtysomething who leads a fulfilling life, and I'm so glad to have time for myself at last. Whereas that time for myself, it terrifies me. I don't know. I expected more from life. It's stupid, isn't it?"

"More what?"

She shrugs. With a wave of her hand she includes the parking lot, the gas station, the bypass, the lights of the town in the background. She says that what she wanted, for example, were moments like the ones we've just had, driving around in the car, miles and miles to kill the night. I sense her voice faltering, but when I raise my hand toward her cheek, she recoils. She asks me why, when we were together, we never had any wild moments like this.

"We had the girls, Anne. They were our wild moments."

She rolls her eyes. She thinks my reply isn't just facile, it's also completely erroneous. We were helicopter parents. The kind who say "be careful" every time either one of them was about to cross the street or climb up on a wall. Demanding parents, too. There were patches of freedom, of course, and that memorable trip to Vancouver and San Francisco—but the rest, all the rest was timed, meticulously organized. We never let ourselves go, completely, as a family, and that's what destroyed us. She lowers her head. She kicks a half-crushed can. She is not blaming me for anything, she says. She is as much to blame for the situation as I am. She also knows by heart all the things people would say to her in reply. How lucky she is to live in the 21st century. In a Western democracy. But still. "But still," she says again.

I take her by the arm. The first glow of dawn is lighting the cathedral, in the distance. I would like to tell her that we will have other sublime sleepless nights, but I know it's just a nice turn of phrase.

ROSE

*H*e looks around, motions to me to follow him, and places his index finger on his lips. Keep quiet. Don't arouse any suspicions. No animals. No ghosts. It is one thirty in the morning. We have broken into the town's cathedral. We intend to climb up to the roof and sleep up there.

He is my first friend, I think.

His name is Thibault, and it sounds ever so exotic to me in comparison to all the boys named Francis, Claude, or Bruno who have filled my childhood. We are seventeen. Thanks to an arbitrary change in the seating arrangement, because of some excessive chattering in French class, Thibault ended up next to me. I was supposed to be the one to calm him down—me, the stereotypical serious, attentive student. The teachers had no idea of the kind of turmoil I was going through. I hid things well. I had become an expert at pretending. Thibault was immediately impressed by my disconcerting ability to follow what was going on in class while scrawling messages to him in my notebook. I can write very legibly with my left hand without ever taking my eyes off the teacher as he scribbles away at the blackboard. Our first exchanges were very factual—"Sure, I'll let you copy all you *want"; "No, that doesn't include doing your homework, what the hell next." Bit by bit we started exchanging gossip about our classmates, but I didn't want to lapse into snitching or facile irony. So we switched to music, movies, and going out. In the weeks that followed we were together more and more often. Some people thought it was an unholy alliance. Opposites attract, said others. They could not imagine how wrong they were.*

"You play your cards close to your chest," Thibault said to me in one of those crowded, smoky cafés in the cathedral district, one Saturday evening after our first two beers.

Inside, I was molten lava.

I met his family, the exact opposite of my own. Young parents, who were never around, a sister who was a die-hard flirt, a welcoming house, but where Thibault, in the end, felt isolated. He has never met my family, or known the stifling, cramped atmosphere of that overheated apartment where the air has trouble circulating.

We make plans. Next year we'll go to Paris. We'll rent a studio; it will be small, for sure, but we'll find a way. We'll make the rounds of every movie theater in the 6th arrondissement; we'll steal new books from the bookstores and borrow older editions from prestigious libraries; we'll sneak into concert halls; we'll meet girls and fall in love with them for three weeks and then wham! Stendhal's vacillations de l'amour, time to change our point of view and our target, we'll be hopeless romantics. Our dreams are sufficient motivation for me to buckle down to work, but I gradually realize that for Thibault it's not the same. The greater the effort we make, the more my grades improve and *his go downhill. He refuses to let me help him. He would feel humiliated, he says. We stop talking about it. We make the most of our newfound popularity. When we navigated through life on our own, we spent our days as solo sailors, but now that we've teamed up, we have been attracting an ever larger crew. A gang has formed. Thibault is captain and I'm first mate. Ever true. Always quick to spot desertion or mutiny.*

And suddenly it's June. Exams. We take our baccalaureate in the same room. I begin to tackle my philosophy essay. I get lost in it. In a trance I see Thibault, sitting in the right-hand side of the room, stand up after an hour and leave. I shrug. It could mean that he's written only two pages but that they are so brilliant he will get a passing grade or even far better. Besides, it's philosophy, and we all know what that means—differences in appreciation, in grading, in approach, all the excuses you can come up with to justify the lack of coherence of your work, its absence of rigor and depth, its fatal clumsiness. I am more worried when the same thing happens for the history-geography exam. I try to get him to look at me; he won't meet my gaze. I phone him that evening, but it's his mother who answers. He doesn't want to be disturbed. Even for me. He is busy revising, she adds. The exam days go by, one after the other. In the very middle of the tests I get a letter telling me that in light of my performance at school I have been admitted to the preparatory classes in Paris I had applied to on the off chance. My parents are pleased, even if they, too, have no idea what it means to get an education at a place like that. I warn them that I'm not sure I'll be able to hack it. In truth, I've already settled on a plan. I will enroll at the same time in the university at Nanterre, to study English or modern languages, I haven't decided which, yet, and I'll quit the elite preparatory classes a few weeks after the courses start, on the grounds that I have too much work, and that the difference between my social background and the other students' feels too demeaning. Thibault, too, will be enrolled at the faculty, in any old degree course. We'll find an apartment to share, which will mean less expense for our parents. Everyone will be delighted. Paris will be our oyster.

On Friday afternoon the written exams are over. Pascaline is having a party. Thibault calls me just before I set out. He's invited but he's decided not to stay for long. He can just imagine what the party will be like, and the predictability exhausts him before he's even been there. He wants me to cut and run with him just before midnight. We could do a bar crawl through the center of town and finally get to talk; he feels as if we haven't really had a proper discussion in weeks. For two seconds I hesitate. I was really looking forward to being with the whole gang tonight. And yet I accept his proposal. I can't imagine saying no to Thibault for anything. At around ten o'clock, when everyone has started dancing and the atmosphere is getting charged, he squeezes my arm and nods toward the front door. We slip out. He seems happy. I'm a lot less so. I find it hard to shift to the rhythm of the city. I would have preferred to stay. We go for a beer at the Café du Musée, right by the cathedral square. I ask him how his exams went, but he sighs and answers that we're not there to talk shop. For the first time, we quickly run out of things to say. We watch the students gulping down colorful cocktails and congratulating one another on their respective alcohol levels. At a given moment, Thibault says, "Come on," and we head outside. It's half past midnight. Clusters of boys and girls are scattered across the square. He leads me to a side street and goes up to a heavy wooden door. In answer to my unvoiced question, Thibault gives me a smile. I grab his arm, he turns around, motions to me to follow and puts a finger on his lips.

And now here we are, the two of us. Sitting with our backs against the tower. Our feet wedged against a gargoyle—a monster from Hell who is baying at the moon. Down below, the city unfurls with all its lights. This is the first time I've come to the top of the cathedral. The door put up only a faint resistance. Thibault picked the lock with a wire he'd brought on purpose. When I asked him how many times he'd already performed this trick, he shrugged and said he liked coming here alone at night, sometimes. Inside, the darkness was hardly penetrated by the glow of streetlamps through the stained glass. Silence. The impression that anything could happen, including the most improbable encounters—mythological creatures, disincarnated angels, genies from a lamp. There was nothing to fear—no one was watching the place of worship. He pushed the padded door that gave onto the stairs to the roof. He held my hand for the first ten steps, the time it took for me to get used to the steep steps and the strange brightness from the moon and the city's neon lights. Halfway up, I glanced through one of the arrowslits. I knew immediately that this scene would root itself in the furthest recesses of my memory. I saw myself in fifteen, twenty, thirty years, on the edge of sleep, recalling the breeze, the lights, the curve of the stone beneath my feet, Thibault's form a little higher up. It brought tears to my eyes.

He could have refrained from talking—I knew what he was going to say. His failure foretold. How we would abandon our impossible dreams, the fantastic Paris we had imagined; we would continue alone down our separate paths. The promises he would not be keeping. The distance that doesn't destroy bonds. Indestructible friendship. Blood brothers. After a while I stopped listening.

I am absorbed in the view. I become one with the streets unwinding before my eyes. I am lost, and yet I am there, intensely present, feeling shivers all down my spine, tension in my shoulders, my eyes almost aching from focusing so hard on the nocturnal city. Thibault has stopped talking. He is looking at me, worriedly. I don't even see him anymore.

I am alone, and yet inhabited by all the paths that open before me, the encounters I'll have, the women I'll fall in love with, the friends I'll embrace, the abysses and summits I'll traverse. When at last I pull my body away from the stone, I am already someone else.

AND THAT WAS IT. He's the one I think of first, as I lie on the red velvet sofa, lost in the contemplation of a chandelier with complicated patterns, each different part meant to refract a strange light when it is lit. I can still clearly see the square outside the cathedral, dimly lit by the orange streetlamps, and the view from up there. The head of the gargoyle cradling my left foot. We could have fallen. Others have. Since that time, access to the tower has been secured. Everything is more secure, nowadays. Cyclists wear helmets, school nurses can no longer dispense medicine, jungle gyms have disappeared from playgrounds. The slightest little thing we say or do makes its way onto the Web.

I am motionless. Not a single muscle is quivering. I am suspended between two eras.

After our climb, nothing was the same between Thibault and me. As he had foreseen, he failed his exams, and he didn't want to try again the following year. He went to work, taking on one badly-paid job after another until he found a permanent position as salesman in a big furniture store. Apparently he likes to tell people that after years in his youth occupying other people's sofas, he has now become a sofa brand ambassador. He adds that it's only fair, and his laughter rings out at parties. He's married. He has a son, Thomas, who is his pride and joy because he's good at tennis, and he continued his studies once he got his baccalaureate. Until Thibault moved to Lyon, three or four years ago, I still got news regularly, through former mutual friends. One of them had brought up my name during one of those men's nights out that Thibault enjoyed so much. He had even insisted, "But you were really close, during the lycée years! Everyone said you were inseparable!" Thibault had pulled a doubtful face and simply replied that adolescent friendships were like love affairs, they came and went, and in the end were not as important as people seemed to think. I still recall the hurt I felt on hearing about this secondhand. So I did not try to get back in touch. I would not have known what to say to him. Other than yes, I do think about him, often. When I glance out the window during a day of classes, or when dawn is breaking over the bypass and as I drive I can see the form of the cathedral against the skyline. For a brief moment, then, I am next to him once again. I can feel the elasticity of my muscles, the tension in my left calf, the city spread before me like a mystery to decipher.

Even today. While the crystal teardrops dangling from the chandelier begin to tinkle—a waft of air moved through the room.

I think about him. Then about Anne. About the coffee we drank that morning after our nocturnal drive, in a bar in the center, just before we went our separate ways again. Her tired face. The way she wouldn't look at me when she talked about her upcoming move to the Southwest. Gujan-Mestras. Gauthier had been offered a promotion, which meant he had to be willing to relocate. Gauthier had let her decide, naturally—she was sure he would have declined the offer if she had asked him to. But she was pleased. This would surely be the opportunity for her to get back in the saddle. New horizons, new faces. It was the reason she had called last night. To say goodbye. Or, see-you-soon, rather, because of course I was welcome to come and visit whenever I liked. I must know that Gauthier enjoyed my company. On condition I never mention our little escapade, of course. I answered with a smile that going around in a loop on a bypass hardly qualified as an escapade. I asked her if the girls knew. She shook her head—no, not yet, but it wasn't really important, deep down, both of them lived so far away. She wanted to tell me first. Because without me they would not be here. Before saying goodbye she mentioned Amélie again. Sang her praises. Divorced. Bubbly. Schoolteacher. A son about to take his baccalaureate exam at the end of the year. She would be at the same New Year's Eve party as Gauthier and Anne herself. There would be a lot of people. It would be great if I could meet her then. I couldn't help laughing. Anne murmured that she wouldn't feel right, moving hundreds of miles away and knowing I was here all alone.

"I'm not alone, you know. I'm even very densely populated."

"Promise me you'll look after yourself."

"That's all I do. It's probably what's wrong with me, anyway. I spend too much time looking after myself."

"Will you think about it, for New Year's Eve?"

"Yes. I don't know what's going on, but this year I'm swamped with invitations. I already have to decide about another party."

"Where?"

"Vienna."

"Vienna?"

"Amazing, isn't it? But I'm not sure I'll go. I'll see."

"And at Christmas?"

"Everything's fine, Anne. Don't worry."

When we hugged, standing in the café, customers suddenly fell silent. They were thinking of their wives, their daughters, their mothers. The warmth of their bodies. I tore myself away from my ex-wife's touch. The day was beginning. And I had a plane to catch.

Now outside, a car is honking its horn. Heated words in German. I keep staring at the glass teardrops hanging from the chandelier. The light is low-angled. Almost snowy. Vienna.

I was twenty years old the last time—the only time—I came here. The 1970s had just come to an end. It was a strange idea, that trip. If you had the means to travel, you went to London, Amsterdam, or New York, lured by what was flashy and trendy. But not her. When I asked where she'd like to go she replied, "Vienna." She added "Austria," and I smiled. Of course I didn't find the destination very tempting. I wasn't that different from the horde of my peers, I wanted vigor, feverishness, overcrowded youth hostels, deafening discothèques, drunken parties with their promise of eternal ethereal friendships. But we'd been together for six months, and I had to admit she'd already made a number of concessions. I wanted to please her, all the more so given the fact that I sensed our relationship was about to end. Around other women I quivered, their bodies more in tune with mine. I didn't realize how pathetic I was being.

She didn't want to fly. Eyes down, she explained that she didn't really like the idea of being catapulted into another world in such a short lapse of time. She needed to feel the miles and the fatigue building up, whereas I dreamed of nothing so much as the roar of jet engines and an abrupt confrontation with another reality. We took the train. The trip seemed endless. She was immersed in a thick English novel from the previous century, with a title that really was not up my alley. *Far from the Madding Crowd.* I tried to lose myself in gazing out at the landscape, but all I could do was make up a mental list of all the parties and dates I was missing out on by temporarily going to bury myself in Vienna. In Austria.

They were strange days. Even today, that week has a place of its own, separate from the mass of my memories. The proprietor of the hotel she had reserved by phone let us choose our room, since at the end of October we were the only customers. The city was blanketed in fog. Gradually my impatience fell away. I was enveloped by the wintery torpor of this capital city that seemed no livelier than a large provincial town. We walked for hours in the cold air. We followed the canal of the gray Danube, so far removed from the idealized image we had had of it. We wandered through the rooms of the monumental museums along the Ring. We shivered in the parks. At the end of the afternoon we made love. Then she would turn her back on me and plunge deep into her novel-reading. She had brought an impressive pile along. She said I could help myself from her personal bookmobile. With great reluctance I started on *Wuthering Heights*. It was during that week, cut off from the rest of the world, while I was getting ready to leave the woman who was there with me, that I fell in love with reading.

Her name was Sylvie. She didn't like her name, she thought it was too ordinary. She would have liked to have been called Constance or Laïla, a name that evoked adventure and dreams. We split up not long after we got back from Vienna. She was far more lucid and clever than I had realized— right from the start she had thought of Vienna as a parting gift. It turned out she couldn't stand me anymore.

I sometimes hear her on the radio. She presents a weekly cultural program. With the other reporters they share their sharp, witty opinions on the latest in literature, cinema, and music. They laugh a lot, volley arguments back and forth. I'm sure that by the end their heads are spinning a little. She has had one of those astonishing career paths that give the lie to all the scornful, wild predictions we might voice, at regular intervals, about the future of the people we meet. In Vienna, we had spoken about the paths that lay before us. She was studying modern literature, but hesitated to go into teaching, because she wasn't sure she could put up with the students in the long run. Pulling a doubtful face, she had mentioned journalism—she had little faith in her ability to break into a milieu where know-how was everything. I read one day in an interview she gave to a magazine that she thought her success was due above all to luck and the people she'd met, when in the end she finally decided to "go up" to Paris, "like a Rastignac crippled with doubts," she had added (and the journalist had added in Italics: *laughter*).

The best decision she made, I believe, was leaving me, when we returned from our Austrian fog. In those days, people expected a lot from me: my parents, my family, the friends I had in those days, my teachers. They thought that "I still had something up my sleeve," or that "I had not yet shown what I was made of." I never really quite understood what it was they dreamed I would become, or what the word "success" implied for them exactly. A royal path toward the mysteries of power? An enduring work of literature? A masterpiece of the cinema? Mountains of banknotes, female conquests one after the other, endless fountains of champagne? None of that happened, but it is of no importance, since there is no one left to bear witness—I don't see any of my friends from the lycée years, my parents are dead, and my teachers are patiently awaiting their spots in the cemetery.

What is important is that I am not disappointed. I have loved my path in life. I have loved Anne, even if we didn't do enough driving around on bypasses at night. I have loved watching my daughters grow up, even if they call only to berate me. I have loved those who have passed through my life and left their mark on me for a few hours, a few weeks, or a few years. I have loved this profession, too. I like to think I was a sun, now and again.

That is why I am here, in a Viennese apartment, on a red velvet sofa. I am evidence of the way I have come, and giving back what was entrusted to me. I absorb and diffract the gray light from outside. I am a crystal chandelier. My memories are tears of glass.

No one knows my address in Austria. No one knows what I am doing here. I have regained the mobility of the invisible.

In a few minutes, Alexandre Laudin will come back. He will recoil imperceptibly when he finds me like this. Even if he is at the origin of the scene. The painting.

I noticed how nervous he was, when we got here a little while ago. He had trouble with the key in the lock. He opened the door abruptly. We quickly took a tour of the premises, just long enough to put down our luggage in our respective rooms, and admire the place as a whole—a caricature of an Austro-Hungarian relic, with heavy drapes, furniture straight out of a museum, imposing chandeliers, all overlooking a cobbled alley leading to a public park. When we came back into the living room, he wanted to close the curtains. Then open them again. I smiled. I ordered him to calm down. We had already talked about it, and I had agreed in principle, had I not? He nodded, a kid caught out. I touched his arm. For a few seconds I felt the electric shock of his youth through my entire body. Insolence regained. I was ready to do battle. I said, "Well? Where?" He pointed with his chin toward the red velvet sofa.

The parquet floor creaked to our every step. I stroked the velvet. With one finger I caressed the curve of the sofa back. I sat down. Timidly at first, on the edge of the cushion on the left; then making myself at home, I spread my arms, open, offered. Alexandre was standing at the entrance to the room, motionless. When he began to speak his voice was toneless. He was familiar with the décor, of course. He had already come here with Tobias, the gallery owner. The same Tobias who had met us at the airport and suggested a quick tour of monumental Vienna, then dropped us outside the building and handed Alexandre the keys, with a gesture of intimacy I did not fail to notice. The two of them knew each other intimately. Tobias had not been surprised to see me. Alexandre had told him I'd be coming. I don't know how he presented me; a former teacher. A friend. A model.

I stared at Alexandre again. I saw the blush seep all the way up his neck and inflame his face. He found it hard to go on. It was here that he had imagined the final painting. He had it in his mind. Of course he hadn't brought any materials, we could not possibly transform this place into a studio, even though Tobias probably would not mind at all, it was his own apartment, a present from his parents on the eve of his eighteenth birthday. A snort of laughter. "He and I don't live in the same world," Alexandre added.

There. He had thought that. Of course, I could refuse. He would never oblige me to. But in his mind it was all very clear. The red sofa. The velvet. My skin.

He was scarlet. I said, simply: "Lying down?"

He nodded.

"And naked, then."

"That's what we agreed. But again—"

I interrupted him with a wave. Now I was the choreographer.

"And how will you proceed? Just sketches?"

"I thought . . ."

The ellipsis spread through the room. Alexandre's eyes were no longer avoiding me. I could sense their presence on my neck, my chin, my mouth.

"I thought, in this case, that I would take photographs."

"You never brought this up before."

"I know. It's an option. Which would have the advantage of only taking a few minutes. Half an hour at the most . . . It would be more . . . more comfortable for everyone . . . In any case for me, that's for sure."

"Comfort is a strange notion for an artist."

"Don't make fun . . . In fact I was thinking about you, above all. Hours of posing is really stressful . . . And besides, it's not my apartment."

"I still don't understand why you wanted this sort of décor."

With his thumb and forefinger Alexandre tugged gently at his eyebrow. There was the ghost of a smile on his face. He replied that even when we unveil ourselves, we are not entirely naked. Each of us is still entitled to an element of shadow, are we not? Well, that red sofa was his element of shadow. He asked me if I agreed, then, to the photographs. I made a face. I said I found the procedure borderline pornographic. And that I didn't want pictures of me, naked, ending up on the web some day. The worldwide one. He hastened to insist that he would destroy them as soon as he no longer needed them, of course he would. That I could trust him. That. Once again I interrupted his flow of words.

"I'll need some time."

He frowned.

"An hour or two. To get used to the idea. To feel at home. Alone."

He instantly understood. He murmured that that was natural, he should have thought of it, he would clear out, leave me some time on my own before he, well, maybe he would go and see Tobias, but why was he telling me all this? One last word, from the doorway. He wanted to know if we could set a precise time. Because of the light, even if today there wasn't a lot of it. Night falls early. Two o'clock? Fine. Fine.

I had ninety minutes ahead of me. I slowly got undressed. I walked around the imposing living room. I cajoled the premises. Tamed them.

I never walk around naked.

The women who have mattered in my life sometimes made fun of my modesty. Of the way I have of turning slightly to one side when I get undressed, and this holdover from adolescence, which compels me to slide hastily between the sheets when it's time to go to bed. I used to laugh about it with them, but I haven't changed my habits. Even alone I don't expose myself. Today is a big first.

In spite of the heat I am shivering. The air wafting through the room caresses my shoulders, prickles down my spine. I readjust my position. For a moment I thought that novelty might lead to desire and its physical manifestations. I was wrong. I am detached from all longing. Removed from time, too. My left arm folded on the armrest. The right one hanging loose. The softness of velvet against my thighs. I recall the odor of leather, in the Highlands, in the car stopped at the top of the hill. The smell of curry in the kitchen near Swiss Cottage. The intoxicating sea air as my daughter and I struggled not to fly away, there on the coast in the Landes. The stone gargoyle beneath my feet, as the nocturnal city opened before me. I am the sum of all those moments. And of the encounters that have shaped me. The chandelier sways gently. In the living room a poorly closed window has just swung open. An icy draft penetrates the room.

Suddenly I stand up. Hastily retrieve my clothes from the floor and put them on. Grab my bag, still unopened. Scribble a note. Crumple it into a ball. I don't need to explain a thing. I am taking back my freedom.

HORIZON

"I THINK THIS IS IT."

"You think or you're sure?"

Clouds scuttle toward the Atlantic. To our left, the jagged mountain covered in lichen and heather. Ahead of us, the road dipping toward one of the many lochs dotting the landscape. I reply that I would stake my life on it. Or his. Anyway, in a few years he won't need it anymore. Alexandre rolls his eyes.

Eighteen months have passed since Vienna. Eighteen months during which we have hardly seen each other. A few weeks after my return, the next-door neighbor knocked at my door. Someone, a man in his forties, had come during my absence. He had left huge packages on the landing. The neighbor thought it was better to take them to his place, for fear they might be stolen. What was more, he wondered what might be hiding underneath the multiple layers of brown paper. "Looks like canvases, don't you think?" I thanked him, but did not answer his uncalled-for questions.

I tore off the wrapping to check what it contained. I looked at myself for only a few seconds. I knew myself inside out. There was no accompanying note. Just a return address. Since the triptych was no longer conceivable, the whole enterprise was null and void. I would never be exhibited in a gallery. I wondered what or who Alexandre would turn to now, but did not dwell on it. I had a life to get started again.

I went to the New Year's Eve party with Anne and Gauthier. I met the famous Amélie, whom I found charming. We had a few evenings together, the four of us, before my ex-wife moved to the Southwest. We got along very well. Once the other two had moved away, my relationship with Amélie deteriorated somewhat, and by mutual agreement we decided to end it. We still call each other now and again on the phone. She has met someone. She is happy. As for me, I recently had a meaningful encounter. I am in the early stages of desire—when you are sussing out the other person, and there seem to be any number of possibilities there before you both. I will soon turn sixty. I can't get over it. I keep my eyes wide open on the path ahead of me.

The paintings were stashed for a while behind the sofa, and then they went to join the rest of the mementoes in the storage room. It's a good place for them, there. I wrapped them back up in brown paper. They help to keep me intact. For almost a year I had no news of Alexandre Laudin. Apparently he was very busy. Living abroad. Moreover, when I went by his building last summer, I noticed a For Sale sign. I never ran into him in the street in town, and I'm glad of that, because I wouldn't have known how to act.

One day, at the station, I saw him on the cover of an arts

magazine. On the glossy paper filled with his face, his chilly gaze contrasted with his fake smile. I read with interest the interview he'd given the journalist. He explained that he was involved in a large-scale project in Vienna. He did not want to say anything more about it, but clearly it was a change of direction. A return to oils, to something almost representative. To the closeness of bodies. He was aware of the risk he was taking, because he was bound to antagonize the viewers who had liked his early work, but risk was inherent in art, was it not?

I dreamed about him one night. People were lining up outside Tobias's apartment, crowded in the stairway. They had all come to catch the eye of the painter. I was not surprised when I heard that, this winter, Alexandre would be having an exhibition at one of the biggest galleries in Paris. The first photos confirmed my hunch. Feverishly painted series of triptychs. Men, women, adolescents, old people, from every corner of the planet. Unembellished portraits of a disorientated world. Fragile and powerful in their exposed nakedness. The painter's eye, said the critics, was both cruel and compassionate—a rare alchemy. I was not invited to the opening.

My daughters are continuing on their way and I am less and less active in their lives. Iris will stay in Canada. She came back last summer without her partner. We went to see her mother and stepfather. It was a fine week, but she had itchy feet—a desire to return to the place she now calls home. Pauline has plans to get married, but she wants to get pregnant first. I found her logic peculiar, but I was careful not to voice any opinion.

I roll the car window down part way. The wind rushes in and the car shudders. I can hear Alexandre breathing by my side. Deeper and deeper. His breath expanding with the view opening before him. The green and gray clashing with red and brown. The forest to our right. The path winding up to the crest. The call of the ocean, which we sense is near.

When I called him, two weeks or so ago, I thought he wouldn't pick up, and that I'd end up leaving a terse message he would quickly erase. Nothing of the sort. He was very happy to hear from me. He wanted us to meet again. I told him what I would like to do. This Scottish landscape, clinging to me. The one I had been thinking about the first time I had posed for him. A desire to be there again. With him. At first he said no, said he had several important appointments; then he laughed, he'd cancel them, of course, they weren't as important as all that, after all. I wanted to know how he was doing. He asked me to send him the electronic tickets, once I had them.

He was waiting at the terminal at Charles de Gaulle and I had a few seconds to observe him without him seeing me. To take in the changes. He has lost a lot of weight. His hair is growing every which way. Something is eating away at him. I hope it is love. I don't really think it is.

He doesn't want to talk about himself. Or about Austria. Or Tobias. Or the new turn to his career. We drove in silence to Kingussie.

I've spent a lot of time on the Internet over the last months trying to find the exact spot. I was about to give up when I came upon some pictures a Dutch tourist had taken. I stared at the screen, transfixed, my body almost frozen. Before my eyes was the very scene from my waking dream, back when Alexandre's pencil was trying to penetrate my mysteries.

I will never know for sure whether it was really the place where Arnaud switched off the engine. I am only too familiar with the sort of traps memory can spring. Remembered images as enticing as they are false. Portraits that seem true to life and which turn out to be utter shams. But I decided I had reached the end of my quest, because everything matched the landscape as I had reconfigured it. The treeless summit. The road sloping ever steeper down into the valley. The loch below. The anthracite rock. The sulfur yellow of gorse bushes. The raw umber earth. The rose and brown of the lichen. And the clouds on the horizon blue.

I roll the windows all the way down.

I murmur, "It's here, yes." I murmur, "Listen."

I release the hand brake.

While the car gradually picks up speed, and the wind rushes into the car, taking our breath away and flattening us against the seats, I think of all those who have left their mark on my life, and of the man who wanted to lay it bare. The road rises up to meet us. Alexandre begins to laugh. When I turn to look at him, he is radiant.

THE 6:41 TO PARIS
BY JEAN-PHILIPPE BLONDEL

Cécile, a stylish 47-year-old, has spent the weekend visiting her parents outside Paris. By Monday morning, she's exhausted. These trips back home are stressful and she settles into a train compartment with an empty seat beside her. But it's soon occupied by a man she recognizes as Philippe Leduc, with whom she had a passionate affair that ended in her brutal humiliation 30 years ago. In the fraught hour and a half that ensues, Cécile and Philippe hurtle towards the French capital in a psychological thriller about the pain and promise of past romance.

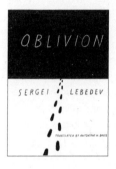

OBLIVION
BY SERGEI LEBEDEV

In one of the first 21st century Russian novels to probe the legacy of the Soviet prison camp system, a young man travels to the vast wastelands of the Far North to uncover the truth about a shadowy neighbor who saved his life, and whom he knows only as Grandfather II. Emerging from today's Russia, where the ills of the past are being forcefully erased from public memory, this masterful novel represents an epic literary attempt to rescue history from the brink of oblivion.

THE YEAR OF THE COMET
BY SERGEI LEBEDEV

A story of a Russian boyhood and coming of age as the Soviet Union is on the brink of collapse. Lebedev depicts a vast empire coming apart at the seams, transforming a very public moment into something tender and personal, and writes with stunning beauty and shattering insight about childhood and the growing consciousness of a boy in the world.

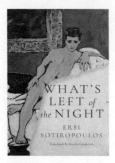

WHAT'S LEFT OF THE NIGHT
BY ERSI SOTIROPOULOS

Constantine Cavafy arrives in Paris in 1897 on a trip that will deeply shape his future and push him toward his poetic inclination. With this lyrical novel, tinged with an hallucinatory eroticism that unfolds over three unforgettable days, celebrated Greek author Ersi Sotiropoulos depicts Cavafy in the midst of a journey of self-discovery across a continent on the brink of massive change. A stunning portrait of a budding author—before he became C.P. Cavafy, one of the 20th century's greatest poets—that illuminates the complex relationship of art, life, and the erotic desires that trigger creativity.

A VERY RUSSIAN CHRISTMAS

This is Russian Christmas celebrated in supreme pleasure and pain by the greatest of writers, from Dostoevsky and Tolstoy to Chekhov and Teffi. The dozen stories in this collection will satisfy every reader, and with their wit, humor, and tenderness, packed full of sentimental songs, footmen, whirling winds, solitary nights, snow drifts, and hopeful children, the collection proves that Nobody Does Christmas Like the Russians.

A VERY FRENCH CHRISTMAS

A continuation of the very popular Very Christmas Series, this collection brings together the best French Christmas stories of all time in an elegant and vibrant collection featuring classics by Guy de Maupassant and Alphonse Daudet, plus stories by the esteemed twentieth century author Irène Némirovsky and contemporary writers Dominique Fabre and Jean-Philippe Blondel. With a holiday spirit conveyed through sparkling Paris streets, opulent feasts, wandering orphans, flickering desire, and more than a little wine, this collection proves that the French have mastered Christmas.

THE EYE
BY PHILIPPE COSTAMAGNA

It's a rare and secret profession, comprising a few dozen people around the world equipped with a mysterious mixture of knowledge and innate sensibility. Summoned to Swiss bank vaults, Fifth Avenue apartments, and Tokyo storerooms, they are entrusted by collectors, dealers, and museums to decide if a coveted picture is real or fake and to determine if it was painted by Leonardo da Vinci or Raphael. *The Eye* lifts the veil on the rarified world of connoisseurs devoted to the authentication and discovery of Old Master artworks.

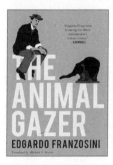

THE ANIMAL GAZER
BY EDGARDO FRANZOSINI

A hypnotic novel inspired by the strange and fascinating life of sculptor Rembrandt Bugatti, brother of the fabled automaker. Bugatti obsessively observes and sculpts the baboons, giraffes, and panthers in European zoos, finding empathy with their plight and identifying with their life in captivity. Rembrandt Bugatti's work, now being rediscovered, is displayed in major art museums around the world and routinely fetches large sums at auction. Edgardo Franzosini recreates the young artist's life with intense lyricism, passion, and sensitivity.

ALLMEN AND THE DRAGONFLIES
BY MARTIN SUTER

Johann Friedrich von Allmen has exhausted his family fortune by living in Old World grandeur despite present-day financial constraints. Forced to downscale, Allmen inhabits the garden house of his former Zurich estate, attended by his Guatemalan butler, Carlos. This is the first of a series of humorous, fast-paced detective novels devoted to a memorable gentleman thief. A thrilling art heist escapade infused with European high culture and luxury that doesn't shy away from the darker side of human nature.

THE MADELEINE PROJECT
BY CLARA BEAUDOUX

A young woman moves into a Paris apartment and discovers a storage room filled with the belongings of the previous owner, a certain Madeleine who died in her late nineties, and whose treasured possessions nobody seems to want. In an audacious act of journalism driven by personal curiosity and humane tenderness, Clara Beaudoux embarks on *The Madeleine Project*, documenting what she finds on Twitter with text and photographs, introducing the world to an unsung 20th century figure.

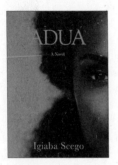

ADUA
BY IGIABA SCEGO

Adua, an immigrant from Somalia to Italy, has lived in Rome for nearly forty years. She came seeking freedom from a strict father and an oppressive regime, but her dreams of film stardom ended in shame. Now that the civil war in Somalia is over, her homeland calls her. She must decide whether to return and reclaim her inheritance, but also how to take charge of her own story and build a future.

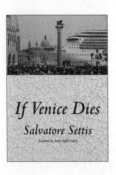

IF VENICE DIES
BY SALVATORE SETTIS

Internationally renowned art historian Salvatore Settis ignites a new debate about the Pearl of the Adriatic and cultural patrimony at large. In this fiery blend of history and cultural analysis, Settis argues that "hit-and-run" visitors are turning Venice and other landmark urban settings into shopping malls and theme parks. This is a passionate plea to secure the soul of Venice, written with consummate authority, wide-ranging erudition and élan.

THE MADONNA OF NOTRE DAME
BY ALEXIS RAGOUGNEAU

Fifty thousand people jam into Notre Dame Cathedral to celebrate the Feast of the Assumption. The next morning, a beautiful young woman clothed in white kneels at prayer in a cathedral side chapel. But when someone accidentally bumps against her, her body collapses. She has been murdered. This thrilling novel illuminates shadowy corners of the world's most famous cathedral, shedding light on good and evil with suspense, compassion and wry humor.

THE LAST WEYNFELDT
BY MARTIN SUTER

Adrian Weynfeldt is an art expert in an international auction house, a bachelor in his mid-fifties living in a grand Zurich apartment filled with costly paintings and antiques. Always correct and well-mannered, he's given up on love until one night—entirely out of character for him—Weynfeldt decides to take home a ravishing but unaccountable young woman and gets embroiled in an art forgery scheme that threatens his buttoned up existence. This refined page-turner moves behind elegant bourgeois facades into darker recesses of the heart.

MOVING THE PALACE
BY CHARIF MAJDALANI

A young Lebanese adventurer explores the wilds of Africa, encountering an eccentric English colonel in Sudan and enlisting in his service. In this lush chronicle of far-flung adventure, the military recruit crosses paths with a compatriot who has dismantled a sumptuous palace and is transporting it across the continent on a camel caravan. This is a captivating modern-day Odyssey in the tradition of Bruce Chatwin and Paul Theroux.

On the Run with Mary
by Jonathan Barrow

Shining moments punctuate this story of a youth on the run after escaping from an elite English boarding school. At London's Euston Station, the narrator meets a talking dachshund named Mary and together they're off on escapades through posh Mayfair streets and jaunts in a Rolls-Royce. But the youth soon realizes that the seemingly sweet dog is an alcoholic, nymphomaniac, drug-addicted mess. *On the Run with Mary* mirrors the horrors and the joys of the terrible 20th century.

The Last Supper
by Klaus Wivel

Alarmed by the oppression of 7.5 million Christians in the Middle East, journalist Klaus Wivel traveled to Iraq, Lebanon, Egypt, and the Palestinian territories to learn about their fate. He found a minority under threat of death and humiliation, desperate in the face of rising Islamic extremism and without hope their situation will improve. An unsettling account of a severely beleaguered religious group living, so it seems, on borrowed time. Wivel asks, Why have we not done more to protect these people?

Guys Like Me
by Dominique Fabre

Dominique Fabre, born in Paris and a life-long resident of the city, exposes the shadowy, anonymous lives of many who inhabit the French capital. In this quiet, subdued tale, a middle-aged office worker, divorced and alienated from his only son, meets up with two childhood friends who are similarly adrift. He's looking for a second act to his mournful life, seeking the harbor of love and a true connection with his son. Set in palpably real Paris streets that feel miles away from the City of Light, a stirring novel of regret and absence, yet not without a glimmer of hope.

ANIMAL INTERNET
BY ALEXANDER PSCHERA

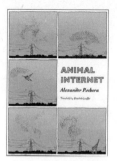

Some 50,000 creatures around the globe—including whales, leopards, flamingoes, bats and snails—are being equipped with digital tracking devices. The data gathered and studied by major scientific institutes about their behavior will warn us about tsunamis, earthquakes and volcanic eruptions, but also radically transform our relationship to the natural world. Contrary to pessimistic fears, author Alexander Pschera sees the Internet as creating a historic opportunity for a new dialogue between man and nature.

KILLING AUNTIE
BY ANDRZEJ BURSA

A young university student named Jurek, with no particular ambitions or talents, finds himself with nothing to do. After his doting aunt asks the young man to perform a small chore, he decides to kill her for no good reason other than, perhaps, boredom. This short comedic masterpiece combines elements of Dostoevsky, Sartre, Kafka, and Heller, coming together to produce an unforgettable tale of murder and—just maybe—redemption.

I CALLED HIM NECKTIE
BY MILENA MICHIKO FLAŠAR

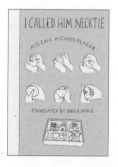

Twenty-year-old Taguchi Hiro has spent the last two years of his life living as a hikikomori—a shut-in who never leaves his room and has no human interaction—in his parents' home in Tokyo. As Hiro tentatively decides to reenter the world, he spends his days observing life from a park bench. Gradually he makes friends with Ohara Tetsu, a salaryman who has lost his job. The two discover in their sadness a common bond. This beautiful novel is moving, unforgettable, and full of surprises.

New Vessel Press

To purchase these titles and for more information
please visit newvesselpress.com.